Alone in his private office, Malik stared unseeingly out at the domes, spires and flat roofs of Teruk's old city. He had a son—a child he'd never, ever been aware of.

A shudder escaped him and he turned from the window. He could hardly believe his grandfather had kept something so monumental from him…even as he acknowledged that Asad's actions, their innate coldness and cruelty, would never surprise him.

And what of Gracie? For a moment he allowed himself to picture her—the tumbling brown hair, the glinting golden gaze, the wide, ready smile. Then he closed his mind to her and all the what-ifs that had ended a decade ago. He could not think of Gracie that way now. He *would* not. No matter what Asad had done, she had wilfully kept his child from him. The only purpose or role in his life for her now was as the mother of his child…and as his convenient wife.

Seduced by a Sheikh

*Two heirs to a desert kingdom
need brides to secure their legacies!*

Brothers Malik and Azim al Bahjat are the two Princes
of Alazar, wielding enormous power with iron control.
They have no interest in love—but duty demands they
take convenient wives, and these ruthless royals
always get what they want!

Read Malik's story in
The Secret Heir of Alazar
April 2017

&

Read Azim's story in
The Forced Bride of Alazar
May 2017

Don't miss this sensational new duet from Kate Hewitt!

THE SECRET HEIR
OF ALAZAR

BY
KATE HEWITT

First Published in Great Britain 2017
By Mills & Boon, an imprint of HarperCollins*Publishers*
1 London Bridge Street, London, SE1 9GF

© 2017 Kate Hewitt

ISBN: 978-0-263-06867-2

Our policy is to use papers that are natural, renewable and recyclable
products and made from wood grown in sustainable forests. The logging
and manufacturing processes conform to the legal environmental
regulations of the country of origin.

Printed and bound in Great Britain
by CPI Antony Rowe, Chippenham, Wiltshire

After spending three years as a die-hard New Yorker, **Kate Hewitt** now lives in a small village in the Lake District with her husband, their five children and a golden retriever. In addition to writing intensely emotional stories, she loves reading, baking and playing chess with her son— she has yet to win against him, but she continues to try. Learn more about Kate at kate-hewitt.com.

Books by Kate Hewitt

Mills & Boon Modern Romance

Moretti's Marriage Command
Inherited by Ferranti
Beneath the Veil of Paradise

The Billionaire's Legacy

A Di Sione for the Greek's Pleasure

Secret Heirs of Billionaires

Demetriou Demands His Child

One Night With Consequences

Larenzo's Christmas Baby

The Marakaios Brides

The Marakaios Marriage
The Marakaios Baby

Rivals to the Crown of Kadar

Captured by the Sheikh
Commanded by the Sheikh

The Diomedi Heirs

The Prince She Never Knew
A Queen for the Taking?

Visit the Author Profile page at millsandboon.co.uk for more titles.

To my fabulous editor, Carly.
Thank you for all your support and input!

CHAPTER ONE

SHE MESMERISED HIM. Malik al Bahjat, heir to the throne of Alazar, watched the girl from afar. She wasn't classically beautiful, but that was part of her charm. Golden-brown hair tumbled down her back in a riot of artless, unstyled waves and curls. Her face was freckled, hazel eyes glinting with humour, with hope, with happiness—three things Malik didn't think he'd ever truly experienced.

She sat on the arm of a sofa, long, golden legs tucked up, wearing cut-off denim shorts and a billowy white top, a pair of bright purple sneakers on her feet. Men were chatting with her, of course—they couldn't keep their eyes off her. No one could. She vibrated with life, with the enjoyment of life, every curve of her lithe body vibrant and sinuous. She was so *alive*.

And Malik had felt like a walking automaton for years, programmed for nothing but onerous duty. He took one step into the room, towards her. He didn't usually go to parties. He was in Rome to assist his grandfather in negotiating a new trade deal with the European Union. Alazar had forged strong links with Europe, links that could stabilise his country's fraught economy as well as the entire region of the Arabian Peninsula.

These meetings were important, Malik knew that; Asad al Bahjat had certainly drilled that into him. Alazar's peace and prosperity rested on meetings such as this one. Then out of the blue a friend from his military schooldays had contacted him, inviting him out, and, knowing how rare such opportunities were, Malik had agreed. One night. One evening where he could act as if he were like other men, as if he had control of his own future, were able to shape his own happiness. Surely he could have that. Surely, after so many years of unquestioning obedience, he deserved it.

He took a step further into the room. Another step towards her. Even though he was still several metres away, she turned, her golden gaze clashing and then tangling with his. It felt like slamming into a wall, leaving him breathless. He didn't want to so much as blink in case he severed the connection.

She looked shocked, her gaze wide and surprised, her full pink lips slightly parted. She didn't blink, either. Malik walked towards her.

He didn't know what he was going to say; he had no chat-up lines. His experience with women was woefully limited, thanks to the security precautions that had been put in place for his own safety. He'd grown up in a palace, with every luxury to hand, but in virtual isolation, save for several rigid years at military school, which had presented their own challenges and difficulties. This was, he acknowledged in wry bemusement, the first real party he'd ever attended. Diplomatic receptions and charity benefits didn't count.

'Hello.' His voice came in a husky rumble; he immediately cleared his throat.

Not a great start, but a smile bloomed across her face that warmed him like a golden ray of sunshine. 'Hello.' Her voice was low and musical.

They stared at each other for a long moment; Malik realised he was grinning. It appeared neither of them knew any chat-up lines.

She let out a soft gurgle of laughter, her eyes alight with humour and mischief. 'Are you going to tell me your name, at least?'

'Malik.' He paused, his mind whirling, spinning with delight at simply being in her presence, basking in the glow of her undivided attention. 'And yours?'

'Grace. But most people call me Gracie. It started when I was a baby and somehow stuck. I tried being Grace for a while, but everyone acted like I was putting on airs. Apparently I'm not the sophisticated type, you know, like Grace Kelly?' She made a rueful face, with laughing eyes. He was enchanted.

Gracie. He savoured the syllables in his mind, in knowing even this much about her. 'I'm pleased to meet you, Gracie. And I like your name just as it is.'

'You have an accent.' She cocked her head, her glinting gaze sweeping over him, affecting him in ways that surprised and unnerved him. She was just *looking.* But he could feel his libido stir, insistent, unforgotten despite years of being ruthlessly reined in. 'But you're not Italian?' It was offered as a question.

'No.'

'What, then?'

'I'm…' He paused. Tonight he did not want to be an heir, a sultan-in-waiting. He'd been that, and nothing but that, since he was twelve years old.

Now that Azim is gone, you must put your childish pursuits aside. You must take his place and be a man.

'I'm from Alazar.'

'Alazar?' Her nose wrinkled. 'I've never heard of it. Is it in Europe?'

'No, the Middle East. I suppose not many people have

heard of it. It is a small place.' And so he dismissed his country, his upbringing and his entire life with a shrug and in that moment he did not feel even a flicker of guilt. 'And you, I am guessing, are American?'

Her eyes danced. 'How did you know? Was it the awful Midwestern twang? I make myself cringe, so I can't imagine how you feel.'

'Your accent is charming.'

She let out a laugh, the sound as rich and full-bodied as the finest wine. 'Now, that's a first. I asked someone for directions this morning and they looked appalled.'

'Then they were both rude and stupid.' She laughed again, and he loved that he had amused her. The knowledge was heady, intoxicating. He didn't need anything to drink, not when he was in her presence. 'What are you doing in Rome?'

'I'm travelling for the summer, before I start college back in Illinois.' She wrinkled her nose again, her smile wry. 'I've always wanted to see the world, something people back home don't really understand.'

'No?'

'No, in fact I think most people back home think I'm crazy.' She adopted a stronger version of her own American twang. 'What do you want to go travelling around the world for, Gracie? It's dangerous out there!' She threw her head back so her hair, in all of its curls and waves, cascaded down her back in a golden-brown waterfall. 'Yep. That's me. Certifiable for wanting to see a little bit of the world.'

'I do not think you are the crazy one.'

'That makes two of us, then.' She grinned. 'So what are you doing in Rome?'

'Business with my grandfather. I am afraid it is most

dull.' He did not want to talk about himself. 'So where are you from in America?'

'Addison Heights. I don't even know why it's called Heights,' she added with another laugh. 'There aren't any. It's as flat as a pancake. Wishful thinking, I suppose.'

'You're different from your friends,' Malik surmised. It was an obvious statement; she was different from everyone. He'd never met someone who shone with such life. He wanted to stand next to her simply to absorb her excitement, her interest.

But no, he wanted more than that. He wanted to touch her silky skin, kiss those petal-pink lips. The realisation shocked him. Sexual desire had been something that had been necessarily shelved for most of his life; now, at twenty-two years old, he felt its overwhelming force.

'Hey, Gracie.' A young man in a wrinkled polo shirt with a pair of beer bottles clutched in one meaty hand shouldered his way towards them. Malik tensed, resenting the intrusion. He was gratified to see that Gracie looked as if she resented it as well, her lips pursing, eyes flashing.

The man gave Malik a wary sideways glance before attempting to edge him out, half standing in front of him, as he handed a beer to Gracie. 'Got your drink.'

'Thank you,' she murmured, and took the bottle but not a sip.

Malik shifted his weight so his shoulder brushed the other man's. The man flinched. At six-three, Malik topped the guy by a good five inches and was heavier and more muscular by several stone. He'd never had to use his size except in training situations, but he discovered he had no compunction about using it now. And neither did Gracie; her eyes glinted again with humour and she smiled, a smile that felt as if it was aimed for him alone, secretive and promising.

'Actually,' she told the man sweating next to Malik, 'I'm not thirsty any more.' She handed him the beer bottle as her gaze swerved to fasten on Malik's. 'What I'd really like is some fresh air.'

'As would I,' Malik returned smoothly. He held out his hand to Gracie, and she slid hers across his palm, causing a tingling, tightening sensation in his midsection.

'Let's go, then,' Gracie said, her eyes sparkling, and Malik led her out of the crowded room.

What was she doing?

Gracie's insides felt as if they were full of leaping, wriggling fish as she followed Malik outside the townhouse in Rome's Trevi district. The June air was warm and balmy, the night full of sounds of city life: the distant buzz of a moped, the clink of glasses and laughter from a nearby café. They stood outside the townhouse, the air caressing their skin like velvet, the mood expectant and alive.

Malik turned to face her, still holding her hand. In the night she could only just make out his eyes, the colour of granite, the proud slashes of his cheekbones. He was the most physically arresting man she'd ever seen. From the second he'd walked through the door, she hadn't been able to take her eyes off him. He was tall, commanding, his broad shoulders and muscled torso encased in a crisp white button-down shirt, his long, powerful legs in charcoal-grey trousers. Next to the motley assembly of college grads and twenty-somethings decked out in dirty jeans and T-shirts, he looked magnificent. Regal. And he'd singled her out for his attention.

A thrill rippled through her. It wasn't like her to be so forward, so bold. She was Gracie Jones from Addison Heights, Illinois, population three thousand. She'd never had a boyfriend, had gone through high school without even being kissed. She hadn't minded; she'd always been waiting for something better, for life to really begin.

Was this it?

'Where do you want to go?' Malik asked. His voice was a low growl that reverberated right through her.

'I don't know. I only arrived in Rome yesterday. I'm as newbie as they get.' She shrugged her shoulders. 'Do you recommend anywhere?'

His faint smile felt like a promise. 'I'm afraid I don't know the city, either. I only arrived yesterday, as well.'

'We're both of us newbies, then.' Although *newbie* didn't seem the right word to describe this man. *Powerful, assured, experienced* were more apt. He was miles above her in every regard.

'How did you end up at that party?' Malik asked.

Gracie wrinkled her nose in a grimace. 'I met that guy with the beers while I was sightseeing. He invited me along, and I thought I might as well go.' She'd been both excited and nervous about diving into a strange and sudden social life, but this was better by far. 'How about we go to a café?' she suggested. 'Get a proper drink?'

His eyes glinted with humour. 'I thought you weren't thirsty.'

'I'm not,' she agreed blithely. 'But we need to go somewhere, don't we?' His gaze held hers and she felt a new heat bloom in her belly at the undisguised desire she saw there. Suddenly she was imagining all sorts of places they could go. All sorts of things they could do...

Which was ridiculous, considering the limits of her experience. And she barely knew this man. She wasn't going to be that stupid, not on her first day in Europe. And yet Gracie couldn't deny the attraction was there, amazingly on both sides, sparking between them. *What would they do with it?*

'I suppose you're right,' Malik murmured. His fingers tightened on hers and he drew her down the pavement, towards a café near the Trevi Fountain, the Palazzo Poli providing a magnificent backdrop.

The pavement café was buzzing with people, but after Malik had a murmured word with the maître d', they were led to a private table tucked in the back with an unobstructed view of the fountain.

Gracie sat down, revelling in the moment, from the fountain lit up from underneath the water, its surface shimmering with lights, to the magnificent palazzo to the even more magnificent man sitting across from her, his silvery-grey gaze fastened on her. She felt as if she had champagne bubbling through her veins, as if every nerve ending was tingling with anticipation.

What was it about this man that made her so excited, so *eager*? Admittedly he was far more handsome than anyone else she'd so much as said hello to, but it was more than that. She felt an understanding with him, an affinity that went beyond a basic attraction to a sexy and desirable man. Or was she simply caught up in the romance of it all? Two days ago she'd been picking at an overcooked hamburger at a family barbecue in dreary Addison Heights and now she was sitting in a café in Rome, swept away by a gorgeous stranger who had, if she'd heard correctly, just ordered a bottle of champagne.

'I love champagne,' she said impulsively. She'd had it only a couple of times, but it had always felt like a decadent treat.

'Good. It seemed appropriate to celebrate.'

'What are we celebrating?'

His gaze didn't leave hers, the heat and intent in it undeniable. 'Meeting.'

'We've barely met,' Gracie protested with a breathless

laugh. Being the unswerving focus of his attention made her feel unsteady, overwhelmed, as if she could topple off the tightrope at any moment. She was nervous, but she was so alive. 'All I know is your name.'

'And where I live.' Malik spread his hands. 'But ask me anything you wish.'

'Anything?'

His eyes blazed into hers. 'Anything.'

Of course, she couldn't think of anything then. Her mind was blank, spinning, her body responding to his, her insides coiled so tightly she felt as if she might snap or explode. She had no room to process anything else.

'Um…' She let out a self-conscious laugh as a blush swept over her. 'How old are you?'

'Twenty-two.'

Twenty-two? He seemed so much older, much wiser and more sophisticated, than she was. He possessed an innate authority, almost an arrogance that both attracted and fascinated her. Had he been born with it, or had he cultivated it? And what on earth did he see in her?

'How old are you?' he asked, and she smiled in semi-apology.

'Nineteen.'

'And you said you are going to college?'

'Yes, in September, to study special needs education.' She'd be heading to Illinois State like everyone else she knew, but at least she was going to live a little first.

Ink-black eyebrows snapped together as he frowned at her. 'Special needs? I am not familiar with this term.'

'Children with learning difficulties and disabilities,' Gracie clarified. 'My little brother, Jonathan, has Down's syndrome and he benefitted so much from good teachers and support. I want to be able to provide the same for other children.'

'That is admirable, to serve for your family's sake,' Malik said quietly. 'I feel the same.'

'Do you?' A dart of pleasure, as well as something deeper, went through her. 'What…what do you do?' The question felt awkward; she knew basically nothing about him. She didn't even know exactly where Alazar was. The Middle East, he'd said.

'I assist my grandfather,' Malik answered. He sounded as if he was choosing his words with care. 'With his various duties and responsibilities. He is…a man of some significance in Alazar.'

'Oh.' Perhaps that explained Malik's dignified bearing. What was his grandfather? Gracie wondered. A diplomat? A businessman? A *sheikh*?

A giggle nearly slipped out at that thought; she felt as if she'd fallen down a rabbit hole into an alternative universe of romance and adventure.

And champagne, for the waiter was bearing down on them with a dusty, expensive-looking bottle and there was no opportunity to ask questions as he popped the cork with a flourish and then poured them two frothing glasses.

'What shall we toast to?' Malik asked as he handed Gracie her glass.

Her mind emptied yet again. 'To the future,' she finally suggested, and then added recklessly, 'To our future.'

Malik's mouth curved, and with his gaze not leaving hers, he raised the glass to his lips. 'To our future,' he repeated softly, and drank.

Gracie followed suit, the bubbles zinging through her, tickling her nose and throat and making her want to laugh. The whole situation made her want to laugh—it was so incredible, so unbelievable. Then all laughter died as Malik lowered his glass and said in a low growl of a voice that pulsed with intent, 'Do you feel what I do?'

Gracie's heart bumped in her chest like a suitcase down a flight of stairs and her hand was unsteady as she returned her glass to the table, barely touched. 'Yes,' she whispered. 'I think I do.' Even if it was crazy.

Malik laughed softly. 'I wonder if I am being fanciful. I do not even know you.'

'No...'

'And yet we have this chemistry.'

'A connection.'

Malik stared at her for a moment and Gracie tensed. Had she presumed...? 'Yes,' he said at last. 'A connection.'

Malik had barely touched the champagne, but he felt awash in it, every sense awakened and buzzing with life. When had he last felt this excited, this energised, this hopeful?

The answer, Malik knew, was never. And yet...

His gut tightened with apprehension. He knew that what he was experiencing with Gracie was temporary, only for a night, if that. His life was not his own to control or decide; it hadn't been since he was twelve, taken from the schoolroom, from his books and model airplanes and the simple life as the second, the spare, thought to be unnecessary. His grandfather's face had been hard, his voice harsh, as he'd explained. *Azim is gone. You are heir now.* Malik had barely been able to grasp his grandfather's meaning, and yet in that one moment his life had completely changed. He'd gone from being a shy, bookish boy who had been left to his own devices to becoming the future Sultan, in the limelight, under the lash, closed off from all the things he'd enjoyed, deprived of the people he'd loved.

But after ten years of resolute duty, surely he could have one evening. One woman.

He leaned forward, needing to touch her, to feel her. Her skin was soft under his hand. 'Let's get out of here.'

Heat flared in her eyes. 'And go where?'

'Anywhere.' He didn't care; he just wanted to be with her.

'We could throw a coin in the Trevi Fountain.' She shrugged, her hair cascading over her shoulders, her eyes alight as her generous mouth curved in a smile that invited him to share in her joy and exuberance. 'Let's live a little.'

Which was exactly what Malik wanted to do—all he could do. *Live*—a little.

'All right,' he said, and rose from the table. He paid for their champagne before heading out into the night, Gracie's hand encased in his. He didn't want to let her go until he had to.

The plaza was full of people and music, and yet it felt as if they were in their own world as they walked by the fountain shimmering with lights.

'Do you know the tradition?' Gracie asked, her eyes full of mischief, and Malik shook his head.

'You're meant to stand with your back to the fountain and throw a coin from your right hand over your left shoulder.' She mimed doing so, her arm reaching over her head in a graceful arc, and Malik enjoyed watching her.

'And then what happens?'

She turned around, smiling at him impishly. 'Then you're meant to return to Rome. But there's another tradition…' She stopped, biting her lip.

Intrigued, Malik arched an eyebrow. 'Another?'

'That you throw three coins in the fountain,' she explained, her voice low. Her face had turned fiery and she couldn't meet his eye.

'Three? What for?'

'One to return to Rome, two for a new romance and three for marriage.' She laughed, the sound a little forced. 'Silly, isn't it?'

Deliberately Malik reached into his pocket. Gracie watched him with wide eyes as he turned so his back was to the fountain and then threw a coin over his head. It landed with a distant splash. Malik threw in another coin. Gracie sucked in a breath.

His heart began to thud as he turned back to face her; she was staring at him, waiting. And so Malik did what he'd been wanting to do all evening. What he'd been needing to do.

He drew her into his arms and kissed her.

CHAPTER TWO

THE TOUCH OF his lips on hers was like a jolt of electricity to her soul. Her whole body flooded with both awareness and need. Her lips parted and his strong hands gripped her shoulders as his tongue touched hers before sweeping into her mouth. Gracie sagged against him, overwhelmed.

Malik broke the kiss, his breathing harsh and ragged as he gazed down at her. From somewhere, Gracie found a wobbly smile. 'That was my first kiss.'

Malik's eyes widened, and then he gave a wry smile. 'Mine, too.'

'What?' Shocked, she pushed herself upright, one hand clutching the edge of the fountain for support. 'How is that possible?'

'How is it not?'

'But you're so…I mean…' She gestured vaguely to his impressive, muscled body. 'You must have had…' She trailed off, too surprised and embarrassed to put it into words.

'I have lived a sheltered life,' Malik stated quietly. 'Out of necessity.' He released a long, low breath. 'Tonight is the first time I've had so much as a taste of freedom.'

'But why…?'

Malik shrugged. 'There are reasons.'

Clearly nothing he wanted to talk about tonight. Gracie

was desperately curious, but Malik's shuttered expression kept her from asking any more questions. 'If this is your first night of freedom,' she said recklessly, 'then let's make the most of it. It's mine, too, in a way.'

'How so?'

Now she was the one to shrug. 'My life has been pretty sheltered, too, living in a small town in Midwestern America. I'm the second youngest of six children, and it was always crazy and wonderful at home, but it meant we didn't have the money for holidays or travel or even eating out. And in any case my parents have always been happy to live and die in Addison Heights. The state fair is the height of sophistication for them. I don't mind, not really, but I've been waiting for adventure my whole life.'

And meeting Malik felt like the greatest adventure of all. She wanted him to kiss her again, right here by the fountain, with all of Rome before them.

Malik must have seen the wish in her eyes for his gaze dropped to her mouth, and as her lips parted, he lowered his head.

'Gracie...' he began, the single word a growling plea. And then he was kissing her and she clutched at the front of his shirt as she drowned in his kiss, everything inside her spinning and straining for more.

Someone nearby let out a wolf whistle and a raucous laugh. Malik tore his mouth from hers. 'Not here...' he muttered, and Gracie's heart bumped again.

'Then where?'

Malik stared at her, his expression fixed as he lifted his hand to stroke her cheek with one finger. 'Would you come back to my hotel room? I have a suite at the Hassler, very near here.'

Her heart was now bumping its way up her throat. She

knew what he was asking. It thrilled and terrified her in equal measure. This had all happened so *fast*.

And yet it felt so right.

It seemed like a cliché, the star-struck traveller falling for a handsome man in a foreign and romantic city. If she'd told her family or friends at home, they'd be either amazed or appalled. Sceptical, too, as they always had been of her crazy dreams.

Travelling, Gracie? But why? Everything you could ever want is right here.

Her parents hadn't left Illinois in over a decade. As for Jenna, her best friend from high school, she wanted only to go to Illinois State and marry her high-school sweetheart. No one had really got Gracie's desire to see more of the world, to live large and to the full.

'Gracie?' Malik stroked her cheek again, making her shiver. 'You don't have to. We can stay here.'

'No, I want to.' She gave him a bemused smile. 'But you remember you were my first kiss, right? I'm not exactly experienced in this type of thing. I don't know…'

'Nor am I,' Malik reminded her. 'I just want to spend time with you. We don't have to *do* anything.'

But when Malik kissed her, she wanted to do all sorts of things. Over and over again.

'Okay,' Gracie whispered, and he led her from the fountain.

Malik's hand nearly shook as he swiped the key card to his hotel suite. He couldn't wait to have Gracie in his arms again. Thank God his grandfather liked his privacy and insisted on them having separate suites. Thank God Malik hadn't encountered anyone but a few sleepy security guards in the hotel foyer. The last thing he wanted right now was his grandfather's icy rage or disapproval.

Gracie stepped into the suite, her eyes wide with admiration. 'This is a lot better than the youth hostel where I'm staying.'

'But now you are here, and this suite is for us to enjoy. So let's enjoy it.' He flipped on some music from the sound system discreetly hidden in a panelled cabinet. The low, sonorous notes of a solo saxophone drifted through the room. Gracie smiled, but he saw the hesitation in her eyes.

With a trembling laugh Gracie swayed a bit to the music. Malik smiled but did not join in the dance. Yet another part of his education that had been neglected. Gracie shrugged as she stopped swaying.

'I don't know what I'm doing,' she admitted, and Malik laughed softly.

'I don't, either.'

'Don't you?' She shook her head slowly. 'It seems hard to imagine. You're so…' she laughed and spread her hands '…fit.'

'Thank you,' Malik said dryly. He'd never really considered his looks either way, except for how he bore himself in public, with the regal dignity required of the next Sultan of Alazar. Yes, if he was honest, he'd noticed a few admiring glances from women, quickly veiled, when he'd been out in public, but they hadn't affected him the way that Gracie's artless confession did. He cared what she thought. What she felt.

And the warmth he saw now in her eyes made him reach for her. She came willingly, breathlessly, her soft, slender body colliding with the hard planes of his chest and thighs and making him ache.

He didn't kiss her, not yet; he wanted simply to savour the feel of her against him, her head tilted upwards and her smile telling him everything he needed to know.

And then, despite his uncertainty, his lack of expertise, the barricades that had been thrown up in every area of his life to keep him safe, he knew exactly what to do. He knew what he wanted to do, and he did it, stroking her face and hair, brushing the tips of his fingers feather-light across the ridge of her nose, the arches of her eyebrows. She exhaled a single, shaky breath.

'I feel like a plateful of jelly.'

'I feel like I am on fire,' he answered, and trailed his finger from the curve of her cheek to the enticing hollow of her throat. Gracie bit her lip, nearly making him groan. He rested his fingertip in the hollow of her throat for another moment before sliding it to the delectable, shadowy vee between her breasts. She let out a soft gasp, and he glanced up to gauge her response.

'Is this...?'

She nodded, her eyes huge, her teeth sunk into her bottom lip. *'Yes.'*

He'd barely begun touching her, and yet already his body ached and throbbed. He could feel the intensity of her response in the way she shuddered, her body taut and straining.

He skimmed his fingers down her front and then slid his hand around her waist, his palm moulding to the dip and curve of her body, fingers spreading and seeking.

Gracie let out a shaky laugh. 'This is so...'

'I know.'

She rested her head against his shoulder, her hair falling across his chest. 'I'm shaking.'

'Are you afraid?'

'No. I just...feel so much.'

'As do I.' He put his arms around her, and they swayed to the music, her breasts brushing his chest, everything in him aching. If he could have held this moment for ever, he would have. It was breathtakingly perfect.

Except being in such close proximity to Gracie made him long for her all the more; he pulled her even closer, their hips bumping, and a soft sigh escaped her. The music ended on a long, lonely note, and Gracie tilted her head up to look at him.

One glance at her heart-shaped face, her lips slightly parted, and Malik had to kiss her again.

Her mouth opened beneath his and one hand clutched at his shirt. He felt as if he could kiss her for ever; he didn't want to do anything else, just lose himself in her lips, in her softness.

Then her hand tightened on his chest and a little moan escaped her, and he realised he wanted so much more than kisses. And so did Gracie.

She pulled away from him a little, her expression dazed, her lips swollen. 'Malik…'

Even though it half killed him to say it, he made himself mutter, 'If you want to stop…'

'Stop? No.' A small, tremulous smile played about her mouth and she shook her head. 'I was thinking the opposite.'

Relief poured through him, along with a tingling, electric anticipation.

'Thank God,' he said, and, taking her hand, he led her further into the suite, and into the bedroom.

In the dim lighting of the bedroom Gracie looked innocent and pure, her eyes wide as she waited for his lead. And despite his own inexperience, Malik knew what to do. What he wanted to do.

He pulled her towards him, his mouth finding hers, his tongue plundering its softness. He skimmed his hands under her shirt, the pleasure of her silky bare skin so intense he sucked in a hard breath. Her breasts were small and perfect, and he cupped them, drawing his thumbs over their peaks. Gracie shuddered.

Suddenly his clothes felt cumbersome. In one fluid movement he pulled his shirt off and Gracie's mouth dropped open slightly.

'Wow,' she breathed, and then laughed softly, self-conscious.

'Can I…?' He gestured to her billowy T-shirt and she pulled it off. Her skin was golden and lightly freckled and Malik ached to explore every inch. Without breaking his gaze, Gracie reached behind and unsnapped her bra, dropping it to the floor. Her breasts were high and proud and perfect. Malik reached out and stroked one with his finger, felt the tremor of Gracie's response.

In answer she placed a hand on his chest, and he felt as if he'd been branded. He pulled her towards him, groaning at the sweet collision of their bodies, and devoured her in a kiss. They moved towards the bed, bodies and mouth intertwining, and Malik lost himself to the most exquisite experience he'd ever known.

I just had sex with a stranger.

Gracie tested the words out in her mind, but they didn't feel right. Malik wasn't a stranger, and what they'd had wasn't simply sex. It had been the most intimate and powerful and frankly amazing thing she'd ever done or felt. And she wanted to do it again rather soon.

But did he? Inexplicably shy considering all the things they'd done, Gracie glanced over at Malik. He lay on his back, his bronzed skin gleaming from their recent exertions, a faint smile on his proud and beautiful face.

Sensing her glance, he turned towards her. 'Are you… Are you all right? You're not…I didn't hurt you?'

Gracie felt a sloppy grin spread over her face. The initial twinge of pain had been replaced by a deeper pleasure than she'd ever known. 'I've never been better.'

Malik's widening smile made her insides leap and writhe with joy. 'I can say the same.' He reached for her again, and Gracie went all too willingly, her body curving deliciously into his, desire and anticipation swirling in her veins like liquid gold, when the sound of the door to the suite being thrown open with force made them both freeze.

'What the...?' Malik began under his breath, but before he could say anything more, a man appeared in the doorway of the bedroom. Gracie registered a stern, autocratic face, a tall, gaunt body swathed in a traditional linen thobe. She shrank beneath the sheets, one hand reaching for Malik, but to her shock he pulled away from her.

'So,' the man said in a cold voice. 'I leave you to your own devices for a single night and this is what happens.' He raked Gracie with a scathing glare. 'You bring some tramp back to your room.'

Malik rolled from the bed in one swift movement, yanking on his trousers before Gracie could even blink. 'Let us discuss this in a civilised manner in the other room.' He didn't even look at Gracie as he bit out, 'You should dress.'

Gracie watched as Malik stalked from the room, preceded by the older man. Her brain felt frozen, her whole body numb. After a few stunned seconds where she simply lay there, the sheet still drawn up protectively over her naked body, she finally forced herself into gear and rose from the bed.

Her whole body shook as she found her clothes and pulled them on, raking her fingers through her tangled hair. A glance in the mirror of the en-suite bathroom showed how wretched she looked—pale face, huge, shocked eyes, hair like a bird's nest. She could hear low, terse voices from the next room, but she had no idea what Malik was saying.

Was he defending her? Explaining to this stranger, who-
ever he was, that he and Gracie had a connection? Somehow Gracie feared he wasn't. Since the awful moment that
man had come in, Malik had seemed like a different person. A hard, cold stranger.

A few minutes later Malik opened the door and Gracie
took an instinctive step backwards at the terribly impassive look on his face.

'You should go.'

That was it? Gracie blinked, opened her mouth and
closed it again. 'Malik...'

'I'm sorry,' he said, his voice flat and his tone not apol-
ogetic at all. 'This was a...memorable evening. But that's
all.' He folded his arms, biceps rippling, drawing Gracie's
gaze even now. 'You knew that.' Had she? What about all
their talk about a *connection*? 'I'll call you a cab.'

A sudden, rolling wave of fury crashed over her. Did
he think he was being generous? 'No, thanks,' she choked
out. She stuffed her feet into her sneakers, not bothering
with the laces. All her focus was on keeping from bursting into tears. She wouldn't give Malik the satisfaction,
and she could certainly do without the humiliation. But
now she had to do the hideous walk of shame, holding her
head high as she walked past both Malik and the older
man, whose malevolent glare could have singed her hair.

'Don't think,' the stranger said, his voice cold and clear,
'that you will gain a penny from selling your story to the
tabloids.'

Gracie turned, her mouth dropping open. 'What...?'

'This is not necessary, Grandfather,' Malik cut across
her. He was glaring at the other man; Gracie might as well
have not existed.

'You are still innocent, Malik,' the man snapped.
'Women like this—'

'Why would I sell my story?' Gracie gasped out, before he could insult her further. 'Who *are* you?'

The man drew himself up. 'I am Asad al Bahjat, the Sultan of Alazar, descended from a thousand years of princes and kings. And you,' he said, his eyes narrowing to nasty slits, 'are nothing but a cheap whore.'

Gracie reeled back at the insult. She looked at Malik, but his expression was unreadable. He said nothing, didn't defend her in any way. Choking on a cry she didn't want to give Malik the satisfaction of hearing, Gracie turned and fled.

'You did not need to be quite so harsh.'

Malik gave his grandfather Asad a level look as the door slammed behind Gracie. The ensuing silence felt like the aftermath of a storm, the emotional wreckage all around them. The emptiness inside him he would not contemplate.

'You do not know what she could have been capable of,' Asad said.

'She did not even know I was heir to the sultanate,' Malik returned. 'She wouldn't have realised there was a story to sell.' Not that he thought Gracie would do such a thing, but he knew he could not afford the naïve sentimentality of such a belief. Not with the weight of the kingdom on his shoulders, the expectation of his role. Dallying with a stranger in a strange city, where anyone could have seen them, had been stupid. Stupid yet wonderful.

And now it was over, as he'd known it would be.

'She would have found out,' Asad scoffed.

'In your arrogance you revealed something that was best kept hidden.'

'Do not think to challenge me,' Asad began, but Malik cut him off.

'And do not think to control me. I am not a boy any longer, subject to your cruel whims. I will be Sultan one day, and one day soon, I have no doubt.' He raked his grandfather with a single look before turning away, furious with both Asad and himself, with the circumstances that had led to this moment. He had always known it would only be a night, but he hadn't wanted it to end like this. And yet how else could it have ended? He had no future with Gracie Jones, American nobody. He hadn't even wanted one.

'Is this what a night with a woman has given you?' Asad scorned. 'A little boyish bravado? You probably think something stupid, like you love her.'

Malik's mouth tightened into a hard line. 'Of course not.' He had no interest in the illusion of love. It had made his father weak, turned him into a hollow wreck of a man, a failure. He would never choose the same for himself.

'You did take precautions, I hope?' Asad asked in a sneer.

Malik swung around to stare at him, his jaw bunched, a muscle flickering in his temple. Asad made a sound of disgust. 'How unbelievably stupid. How like your father, putting sentiment and romance above basic practical concerns.'

'I am not like my father,' Malik snapped. 'In any regard.'

Azim shook his head. 'If only Azim had lived. We would never be in such a state as this...'

It was a lament Malik had heard often over the last decade, and one he had no patience for now. If only Azim had lived, the older brother, the true heir. Over the years Asad had built up Azim into a hero, the fourteen-year-old boy stolen from his youth who would have been the perfect heir, the rightful Sultan, unlike Malik, who was there in proxy, an unwanted second choice, too like his father, according to Asad. Soft. Weak.

Asad had done his best to mould Malik, sending him to military school, beating duty into him whenever he could. Malik had learned the lessons all too well, but he refused to be cowed now. Not this time. Not ever again. Perhaps that would be the legacy of his one night with Gracie.

'Alas, he did not live,' Malik said coldly. 'And there is little we can do to change matters at present, unless you have powers I am unaware of.'

'And if she's pregnant?' Asad demanded. 'Have you considered that?'

Malik clenched his jaw, hating that his grandfather had caught him out. If Gracie was pregnant... Why had he not considered such a possibility? They'd both been so inexperienced, so overwhelmed by passion.

'The possibility of her pregnancy is extremely unlikely,' Malik said with more conviction than he actually felt. 'But if she is, I am sure she will attempt to be in touch and I will handle the matter then.'

'How?' Asad demanded. 'By parading your bastard child in front of the press? By polluting a thousand years' lineage of princes and kings with some American half-blood brat?'

'That is enough,' Malik snapped. He took a deep breath and released it slowly. 'I will do what I feel is best.'

'You do realise how this kind of publicity could affect our country?' Asad demanded in a low voice. At that moment he looked every inch his seventy-six years, uncertainty and genuine fear flickering in his faded eyes. 'Our trade agreements, our relationships with the Bedouin tribes...everything is built on the bedrock of a stable monarchy. Alazar is a traditional country. They cannot have a sultan who acts like a Western playboy. If you do anything to make people doubt or wonder...'

Malik nodded, a terse assent of all his grandfather had

both said and implied. He knew his duty, and he would fulfil it. He would not shame either himself or his country by chasing after a slip of a woman, even if she had possessed more life and given him more joy than he'd ever known. 'I will not, Grandfather,' he said quietly. 'I will never.'

Rome had lost its magic. Back at the youth hostel where she'd left her bags what felt a lifetime ago, Gracie showered and changed. She shouldered her backpack and paid for her accommodation before heading out into the sultry, suffocating heat of a summer's day. What had been beautiful and wondrous a day before now looked dirty and crowded.

A moped sped by her in a gust of diesel and someone pushed her shoulder hard. Gracie stumbled back a few steps before righting herself. Taking a deep breath, she hefted her backpack more securely on her shoulders and started walking towards the Termini rail station.

By mid-afternoon she was in Venice and had secured a place in a new hostel. She wandered along the Grand Canal, wanting to be captivated by the magic of the beautiful, crumbling city with its many canals of blue-green water and yet utterly unable to. Inside she felt both leaden and numb, filled with the memory of how Malik had pushed her away from him, told her to leave, his expression so cold, almost contemptuous...

There had been no *connection*. He probably used that line on every eager woman he saw. And as for his confession that it had been his first kiss? Laughable. She should have seen through that immediately. He'd kissed her with far too much expertise and assurance to be as inexperienced as she was. He'd known how to touch her from the first.

Added to all that, he was the heir to a *kingdom*. A man of some significance, he'd called his grandfather. As if.

Clearly he'd been doing nothing but amusing himself with an American bumpkin. She was so *stupid*. Stupid and naïve.

Gracie trudged through another few weeks of travelling, but the joy and sense of adventure she'd had when she'd started out had left her completely. All she wanted to do was hightail it home, to a place where people knew and loved her. But then the thought of all the triumphant I-told-you-sos from friends and family who hadn't seen the point of her going at all was enough to stiffen her resolve. She would get over Malik al Bahjat, heir to the throne of Alazar. It wasn't as if her heart had been destroyed. Just her pride, she assured herself, along with her innocence.

Then, in a tiny village in Germany, with rain sleeting down over the Black Forest, she threw up her breakfast. She rested her head on the edge of the toilet, her stomach still heaving, the noisy sounds of the hostel echoing around her. Cold sweat prickled on her scalp and she closed her eyes. The last thing she needed was the stomach flu while backpacking through Europe.

Then she threw up the next morning, and the morning after that, and her breasts started feeling tender, fatigue crashing over her at every opportunity. It took another week for Gracie to realise the appalling, obvious truth: she was pregnant.

CHAPTER THREE

Ten years later

'I'M SORRY, YOUR HIGHNESS.'

Malik looked up as the doctor entered the examining room and he narrowed his eyes. 'Pardon?'

'The results of the test were conclusive.' The doctor, a dour-faced man who had been medical consultant to generations of royalty, lowered his head. 'You are infertile.'

Malik's expression did not change as the words reverberated through the emptiness inside him. 'Infertile,' he repeated tonelessly. The doctor looked up.

'You had a sustained high fever while you were out in the desert. It is a situation that can unfortunately, in rare cases, cause infertility.' He lowered his head again, as if waiting for Malik to pass sentence.

But there was no sentence for him, only for Malik. A life sentence, or lack of one. He was the only heir to the sultanate of Alazar, and he had no heir to succeed him. No way of getting an heir in the future. His engagement to Johara Behwar, a young woman of virtue and suitably elevated background, had just become a pointless sham. And the stability of his country, a country that had teetered on the edge of civil war for the last ten years, was once again in jeopardy.

Underneath all those political concerns was a deeper, more personal sense of loss that he could not bring himself to probe. Malik turned away from the man to compose himself and gather his thoughts. 'You are quite sure?' he asked after a moment, the words clipped and terse.

'Quite sure, Your Highness.'

Briefly Malik closed his eyes. He'd spent two weeks with the Bedouin in the bleak and arid deserts of Alazar's interior, trying to unify and encourage his people, and keep the peace that had threatened to topple into chaos and destruction. He had succeeded, but the cost had been high. Too high.

In truth he barely remembered the fever that had stolen his future from him. He'd been delirious, kept in a rough tent and administered to by a Bedouin Hakim, whose knowledge of local herbs and natural medicine had not been enough to lower the fever. Eventually the Bedouin had moved him to a nearby settlement where his grandfather had arranged transport to a medical facility in Teruk. By then he'd had the fever for four days. Long enough, it seemed, to render him infertile.

For a second, no more, Malik allowed himself to experience the grief of knowing he would have no children. No heirs. No children to follow him, no hearts and minds to shape.

The second passed and Malik steeled himself. He had no space in either his life or heart for such useless sentiment. He hadn't for a long, long time. Love was weakness, and he could not afford to be weak.

'Thank you for telling me,' he said with a nod of dismissal. The doctor left, and Malik strode from the room. He would have to tell his grandfather.

He found Asad in one of the smaller throne rooms, dealing with some paperwork. For a moment Malik stood in the doorway, noting the many wrinkles in the old man's weathered face, the way his hands shook a little as he handled some papers. Asad was eighty-six years old and he showed every year in his body and on his face.

Over the last ten years Malik had assumed more and more responsibility for the running of Alazar; Asad had been unable to cope with the travel and diplomacy that the country's wavering instability had required. Malik had spent much of the last decade on horseback or in a helicopter, travelling through arid deserts and unforgiving mountains, living in rough conditions and negotiating with people who had the power to cause major civil disruption. Slowly but surely he was dragging Alazar into the twenty-first century while still attempting to respect the old ways and traditions. His marriage to Johara, along with his future heirs, would have cemented his power and the security of the sultanate as well as the whole of the Arabian Peninsula.

But now? How would the traditional Bedouin who controlled much of the country's desert and mountain regions react to an infertile sultan, the line of succession passed to some distant relative who had no training or reputation? His stomach cramped just thinking about it.

'Well?' Asad demanded as Malik came into the room. 'What did the doctor say? You have not been adversely affected by the fever?'

Malik took a deep breath, steeling himself for a conversation he had no desire to have. 'As it happens, I have been affected.' He shoved his hands into the pockets of his Western-style trousers; unlike his grandfather, Malik saw the necessity of adopting Western ways and bringing Alazar into step with the rest of the world. He kept his voice even as he clarified, 'I'm infertile.'

Asad's mouth worked for a moment, shock making his eyes bulge. 'Infertile? But how...?'

Malik stared at his grandfather's pale face and felt nothing. But then he hadn't felt anything in years. He'd been completely focused on his country and his duty; he'd had to be. There had been no room for entertainment or pleasure or relationships. He hadn't wanted them. 'Apparently a prolonged high fever can cause infertility.' He shrugged, the movement negligent, as if it were of little consequence even though they both knew it was not. 'The how does not matter so much, does it?'

'I suppose not.' Asad was silent and Malik wondered what the old man was thinking. Where did they go from here? Azim was dead; Malik was the only heir. If he had no son, the sultanate would go to a cousin in Europe who had spent very little time in Alazar. Someone who could not be trusted to maintain the country's stability. Someone who had not been working towards ruling since he was a boy, who had not, out of necessity, cut off pleasure and leisure and love as Malik had.

Asad sat back in his chair, his face drawn into a frown, his gaze distant. 'This presents a problem,' he murmured, almost to himself.

Malik let out a harsh laugh. 'Thank you, Grandfather, for stating the obvious.'

Asad looked up, his narrowed eyes gleaming with familiar malice. 'As it happens, there is a solution.'

Malik stared at him evenly. 'Which is?' He could not imagine any solution. He could not magic a child out of nowhere, much as he might want to, and he did not think his grandfather would try to put him aside for some unknown relative. Not after ten years of tireless work and effort.

Asad took a slow, steadying breath. 'You have a son.'

Malik stared at him blankly. 'What on earth are you talking about? I would know if I had a child.'

'Would you?' Asad asked shrewdly, his gaze both knowing and sly. Malik didn't even blink. Yes, he would know. He'd had a mere handful of one-night stands over the last ten years, matters of physical expediency rather than lasting pleasure, and he'd always been careful with birth control. There had been only that one time...

Malik stilled, suspicion icing in his veins, disbelief coursing through him. 'What are you saying?' he asked, a command rather than a question, each word savagely bitten off and flung out.

'The girl in Rome.' Asad pressed his lips together. 'She was pregnant.'

The girl. *Gracie*. He hadn't let himself think of her at all in the last ten years, not even for a single, bittersweet second. At first it had been a form of extreme mental self-discipline, bordering on torture, not to allow himself so much as a thought, a tempting fragment of memory to tease his senses and awaken the old, restless ache. After a while the pain had lessened and she'd been like a ghost, some-times haunting his dreams but never his waking thoughts. She belonged in his past, with the naïve, hopeful boy he'd been then. She had no place in his present, and certainly none in his future. Until now.

'Pregnant,' he repeated, his tone silkily dangerous. His hands clenched into fists at his sides and he forced himself to relax. 'She came to you, I presume, with the information? Looking for me?' He could picture it.

'She sent an email to a government address and it was brought to my attention. I met with her in Prague.'

'For what purpose?' Rage choked him, made it hard to speak or even breathe. 'You didn't think to tell me any of this?'

'You didn't need to know.'

'I should have been the one to decide that.'

Asad shrugged, unrepentant. 'You know now.'

Malik forced himself to breathe evenly. He knew from far too much experience that arguing with his grandfather served no purpose. There were other ways to best the old man. 'So what happened in Prague? You sent her away, I presume?'

'I bought her off. Fifty thousand dollars.' Asad's mouth twisted in contempt. 'She took it readily enough.'

'Did she?' Malik could not assess how he felt about that. He had not thought about Gracie in so long he didn't know how he felt about any of it. She'd been *pregnant*. And she'd had no compunction about not letting him know.

'She cashed the cheque the next day,' Asad continued. 'And she had the child. A son. I checked.'

Malik turned away to hide the betraying emotion he was sure would be on his face. A *son*. He could not even fathom it. Gracie had been raising his son for ten *years*. 'How could you keep this from me?' he demanded in a low, raw voice.

'Don't be a fool. Of course I had to keep it from you. The publicity would have damaged your reputation as well as the stability of the kingdom. The boy is a bastard, his blood is tainted.'

'He's *mine*—' The words rose up in him, a raw, primal howl of possession that shocked him with its ferocity. He'd never felt anything like it before.

'He is your heir,' Asad agreed coolly, cutting him off. 'Now. And for that reason you must secure his future and bring him back to Alazar. Let us hope he has not been too weakened by his lax upbringing. There is time to shape him yet.'

'And what of his mother?' Malik demanded.

Asad's mouth twisted. 'What about her?'

'She might not agree.'

'She will have to. In any case your heir cannot be a bastard. You will have to marry the woman.' Asad spoke with distaste, even as Malik felt a pulse of—what? He could not identify the emotion. Excitement, perhaps. Desire. Even after all these years. He pushed the feeling away. He had no time for it now. Any marriage he contracted would be one of expediency, not emotion. He would not be controlled by feelings the way his father had, to his shame and destruction.

'The people might not accept an American bride and heir,' Malik observed.

'Then you will have to put her away somewhere remote.' Asad flicked his fingers in a dismissive gesture. 'Keep her in purdah in one of our distant palaces. Whatever the cost, you must do your duty.'

'You do not need to remind me,' Malik answered, 'or tell me what to do.' He straightened, giving Asad a long, level look. 'I will make my own choices,' he said, and walked out of the room.

Alone in his private office Malik stared unseeingly out at the domes, spires and flat roofs of Teruk's old city. He had a son, a child he'd never, ever been aware of.

A shudder escaped him, and he turned from the window. He could hardly believe his grandfather had kept something so monumental from him, even as he acknowledged Asad's actions, their innate coldness and cruelty, would never surprise him.

And what of Gracie? For a moment he allowed himself to picture her, the tumbling brown hair, the glinting golden-green gaze, the wide, ready smile. Then he closed his mind to her and all the what-ifs that had ended a decade ago. He could not think of Gracie that way now. He would not. No matter what Asad had done, she had wilfully kept his child from him. The only purpose or role in his life now for her was as the mother of his child...and as his convenient wife.

'What's the capital of Mongolia?'

Gracie wrinkled her nose as she considered the answer and then came up with nothing. 'Sorry, Sam, I have no idea,' she told him cheerfully. 'But I'm sure you'll tell me.'

'Ulaanbaatar,' he said triumphantly, and Gracie suppressed a smile. Her son had an insatiable knowledge for facts and was constantly begging her to quiz him. When she ran out of questions to ask, he started quizzing *her* and left her both amazed and humbled by his knowledge.

'Teeth and bed,' she said now, and with a dramatic sigh Sam rose from the table in their small kitchen. For the last ten years Gracie had been living in the converted apartment over her parents' garage. A tiny kitchen, living room, and two bedrooms and a bathroom were all it comprised, but it was homey and hers and she was grateful to her parents for giving her the opportunity.

Ten years ago, when she'd told them she was pregnant, and by a near stranger at that, they'd been shocked and, yes, disappointed. But they'd rallied around her and Sam, and she'd never once regretted her choice. If she occasionally wished for some way to flee the sometimes stifling confines of her life—well, that was normal, wasn't it? Everyone longed for adventure once in a while. It didn't mean she wanted out.

And there was no out, because she needed her part-time job as a classroom assistant at the elementary school, just as she needed her parents' support, even if it came with the occasional sigh or frown, and the knowledge that out of six children she was known as 'the Jones screw-up'.

The girl who'd gone to Europe and come back pregnant—
a warning to any other dreamy teens who might hope for
adventure the way she had.

While Sam got ready for bed, making a ton of noise as
he did so, Gracie tidied the kitchen, humming under her
breath. From the window over the sink she could see the
white clapboard house she'd always called home, with its
bowed front porch, American flag, and neat flower beds
of begonias and geraniums.

Her parents had been incredibly thoughtful about giving Gracie her own space, but the reality was she was living in her parents' backyard. It wasn't exactly where you
wanted to be when you were staring down the barrel of
thirty years old.

Still, Gracie reminded herself as she wiped the table and
turned on the dishwasher, she was better off than some.
She had a job she enjoyed, a home for her and her son, a
few friends who she went out with on occasion. If life felt
a little quiet, a little dull, well, so be it. Plenty of people
felt the same.

She'd just put Sam to bed when a gentle knock sounded
at the front. 'Gracie?' Jonathan called.

'Hey, Jonathan.' Gracie opened the door to see her
brother standing on the top step of the outside staircase,
a worried frown on his usually smiling face. 'Is everything okay?'

'There's someone here to see you.'

'There is?' Gracie didn't get too many visitors at home.
Since her apartment was so small, not to mention so close
to her parents' house, she tended to meet her couple of
girlfriends in town. 'Do you know who it is?' she asked.
Everyone pretty much knew everyone in Addison Heights.

Jonathan shook his head. 'I've never seen him before.
But he's kind of scary-looking.'

'A scary-looking man is here to see me?' Gracie didn't know whether to be amused or alarmed. She supposed Keith at the service station was a little bit scary-looking. He'd asked her out last week and she'd firmly rebuffed him. She wasn't interested in dating, and certainly not Keith, not with Sam to consider. She didn't think the mechanic would actually come to her house, though.

'Well, I'd better go see who it is,' she said lightly, and rested a reassuring hand on her brother's shoulder. At twenty-seven, Jonathan lived at home and worked part-time bagging groceries at a local supermarket. He also spent several afternoons at a care facility for adults with disabilities, and, while he was more than content with his life, change or uncertainty made him nervous. And the last thing Gracie wanted was for Jonathan to be nervous.

They walked across the yard just as dusk was beginning to fall and the crickets started their incessant chorus. It was early June and already hot, although the twilight brought some needed cool. Gracie came around the corner of the house and then skidded to a complete halt when she saw the man who stood, or really loomed, on her parents' front porch.

Malik.

He looked incongruous amidst the begonias and white weathered wood in his dark suit, expensively cut and tailored. Utterly forbidding. His face was unsmiling and severe.

He turned to look at her, and for a single second the whole world felt suspended, transformed. Gracie felt as if she'd catapulted back in time a decade; she could almost hear the buzz of a moped, the tinkle of water as they stood by the Trevi Fountain and Malik threw a penny over his shoulder...

Then she landed back in reality with a thud so hard it

left her breathless. No, they weren't in Rome, caught up in an impossible, ridiculous one-night romance that hadn't been real anyway. They were in Addison Heights, and it was ten years on, and everything had changed, even if for a few seconds she'd felt as if it hadn't.

But why was he here?

'Malik…' she whispered, and found she couldn't say anything else.

'You know him, Gracie?' Jonathan asked. He was looking at Malik with unabashed curiosity. Yes, she acknowledged distantly, Malik *was* kind of scary-looking now.

Malik's gaze snapped to focus on Jonathan. 'This is your brother. Jonathan.'

His voice was the same, a gravelly husk, and it reached right inside Gracie and squeezed. And then came an even more painful realisation: he *remembered*. How…? *Why?*

'Yes,' she managed, her voice barely a breath. 'Malik, what…what on earth are you doing here?' It felt strange to say his name, and she saw the answering awareness flare in his own eyes. Memories tumbled through her, painful and sweet and shockingly fierce. Laughter and kisses, dancing in starlight, holding hands… Gracie took a deep breath. 'I never expected to see you again.'

'So you hoped.'

She blinked at the cold remark. *What…?* And then she realised. He knew about Sam. Of course he did. And she had no idea how she felt about that.

Jonathan tugged on her sleeve. 'What's going on, Gracie?'

'This is just…just an old friend, Jonathan. We, ah, need to talk in private.' Gracie tried to smile at her brother, but her face felt funny and stiff. If Malik was here because of Sam…*what did he want?*

She watched as her brother eyed them uncertainly before climbing the weathered steps of the front porch and disappearing inside.

Gracie looked back at Malik, her eyes memorising and remembering him at the same time. Those long, power-ful legs. The broad shoulders. The silvery, intense gaze, the kind smile… Except he wasn't smiling now. He hadn't smiled since she'd seen him here. His face was as inscrut-able and unyielding as a statue's, beautiful and so very cold.

'We can't talk out here,' she said.

'Is there somewhere private?'

As reluctant as she was to invite him into her tiny home, Gracie couldn't see any other option. She couldn't leave Sam alone for too long. 'I live around the corner,' she said. 'We can talk there.'

Malik inclined his head in a terse nod and Gracie turned to head back to her apartment. Malik followed, pausing only when she reached the front of the garage.

'You live in a garage?'

'Above it. There are stairs around the back.' She led him to the outside staircase that ran along the wall. Her hands were shaking so much she fumbled with the knob before it swung open and she breathed a sigh of relief.

Malik stepped into her cosy kitchen, his tall, broad form making the small space seem even tinier. He looked so out of place amidst the colourful riot of houseplants, the cheerful yellow walls. Gracie retreated to the sink, its edge pressing into her back. She had no idea what to say, to think, to feel. Malik…*here*. It felt impossible, ridiculous. Exciting, too, which annoyed her. There was nothing to feel excited about, even if seeing Malik again made her re-member so much. Want so much, even if it was foolish. *He pushed you away,* she reminded herself. *He told you to go.*

Malik folded his arms, the movement seeming one of forbidding judgement. 'You should have told me.'

'About what, exactly?' She folded her arms and met him with as challenging a look as she could muster. She wouldn't be cowed by this cold, haughty attitude. 'Maybe you should have told me you were a sultan.'

'Heir to the throne,' he dismissed, and she let out a laugh that sounded a little too high and wild.

'Oh, *okay*, then.'

Malik arched an eyebrow in an eloquent gesture of silent incredulity. He was so different than she remembered. Yes, he was just as devastatingly attractive, but he was colder now. Sharper, too, and more hidden. Remote and unreachable, without the warmth and friendliness, the tenderness that she'd once revelled in. Except that had all been an act, she reminded herself. This was the real Malik. He'd shown his true colours when he'd kicked her out of his bed.

'Don't play me for a fool a second time, Grace. You know what I'm talking about. My *son*.'

The *Grace* hurt. She was Gracie. He knew that. And as for his son… Sam was *hers*.

'I never played you for a fool,' Gracie replied. Her voice thankfully came out cool, if not as cold as his. 'If anyone was tricked, it was me.'

'With fifty thousand dollars in your pocket?'

Colour and heat flared in her face. So he knew about the cheque Asad had thrust at her. He must have learned everything, no doubt from Asad. But why? His grandfather hadn't wanted Gracie, cheap tramp that he'd thought her, in Malik's life. Why tell Malik now? Or had he discovered it on his own? And why did she now feel guilty for taking that money?

When Asad had found her in Prague just hours after she'd sent a desperate email to an anonymous government address, she'd been both shocked and afraid. He'd bundled her into his blacked-out sedan and told her point-blank to get rid of the baby. When, horrified, she'd refused, he'd handed her the cheque with the stipulation that she never contact anyone in Alazar again.

Gracie had been so overwhelmed, so *frightened*, that she'd signed the paper he'd waved in front of her nose and taken the cheque. And yes, she'd cashed it. She'd considered it eighteen years of child maintenance payments. And she'd needed that money, for both her and Sam's independence. It had enabled her to stay at home with him until he'd started school.

'Why don't you tell me what you know?' Gracie suggested, her voice wobbling only slightly.

Malik let out a sharp bark of contemptuous laughter. 'Hedging your bets?'

'It would make for an easier conversation,' Gracie returned, an edge now entering her voice. She could tell already that in the decade since she'd seen him last, Malik had painted her in the same colours that his grandfather had. Perhaps he'd always seen her that way, as the cheap whore Asad had branded her.

The realisation hurt, which was ridiculous, because she knew she shouldn't care what Malik thought. But she hated being judged, especially when it was so patently unfair. Enough people in Addison Heights had judged her for having a baby as an unwed mother. She didn't need it coming from Malik, as well. She'd shown him her true self, something he'd either forgotten or disbelieved.

'Fine,' Malik returned. 'I'll tell you what I know. I know after our night together you became pregnant with my child. I know you sent an email to a government address. I know my grandfather found you and offered you fifty thousand dollars for you to go away. I know you took it.' His gaze was icy with contempt as he glanced around the kitchen. 'Perhaps you should have held out for more.'

'Fine,' Gracie parroted him when she could trust her voice. She was torn between screaming and bursting into tears. After ten years of trying to make a life for herself and Sam, he reduced her to this? A money-grubbing tramp who hadn't even been able to cut a good deal. 'So you know all that. Now, what do you want?'

'My son.' The two words were spoken with such un-relenting authority that Gracie nearly jumped. Then she stared.

'You want your son? Just like that? After ten years of absolutely nothing?' She was trying to sound coolly in-credulous, but her voice wobbled all over the place. In truth she was terrified. Asad's icy dictates felt as fresh as they had when she'd been sitting in his sedan, the door locked, the old man's face stonily impassive. Except now it was Malik giving the commands, his face that looked so cold and unyielding, and it felt far worse. Far more frightening.

'Yes, just like that,' Malik returned. 'I only learned about his existence three days ago. You've had him for ten years.' His expression didn't so much as flicker as he added implacably, 'Now it's my turn.'

CHAPTER FOUR

MALIK WATCHED GRACIE'S face pale as her slender body swayed and he knew he should have been gentler, more persuasive. The trouble was, he didn't know how to be that any more. Ten years of living in a battle zone left a mark. And in any case he had neither the patience nor the time to woo this woman. He would take what he needed no matter what.

Still, he knew it wouldn't do to frighten Gracie off before he'd even begun. This required careful handling. He took a deep breath and let it out slowly.

'I need to see my son, Gracie.' The old name slipped out before he realised, and he saw that she noticed. A welter of confusing emotions rose up in him, and he forced them all down. He could not let himself be clouded by sentiment. Not now, not ever. He was *not* his father.

'Malik…this is such a shock.' She pressed her hand to her chest. 'I never expected to see you again. Your grandfather made it very clear I was to disappear.'

'Which you were happy enough to do.'

'Happy? No.' She shook her head as she bit her lip, her face still pale. 'But it seemed the best option, considering. In any case you can't just bulldoze into our lives like this…'

'You'll find I can,' Malik stated. A latent anger thrummed

under his words, and he saw Gracie register it. 'You never should have kept him from me.'

Temper flared in her eyes. So she was angry, too. Fine. 'I didn't have much choice.'

'There is always a choice.'

She shook her head slowly. 'So you've decided to paint me as the villain in this melodrama, despite the fact that I *tried* to contact you and your grandfather is practically insane. *And* you want me to just hand over my child like he's some parcel you can collect when you feel like it. Great. Really great.' She shook her head again as her arms crept around her body and she hugged herself. He could see how her body trembled and shook, and he felt a flicker of pity.

'Let us try to discuss this reasonably, Grace.' He tried to moderate his tone, even though he felt lit up like a stick of dynamite inside, with every word acting as a match to tinder. Anger and regret churned within him; the explosion was only a matter of time. He had a son he'd never known about, never been given the chance to know. The fault was Asad's—and also Gracie's. 'You must see I have parental rights.'

'Ye-es,' Gracie admitted, the word drawn from her reluctantly. 'But so do I.'

'Then let us find a way forward.' He was going to have to handle her very carefully, Malik could see. She would resist his ultimate intention: to bring both her and the boy back to Alazar. As for marriage…that would come in time. He had no intention of admitting all of his plans to her now, in the heat of their meeting. Who knew how she would react, what she might do? He needed her cooperation, preferably her docility.

Gracie pressed a hand to her head. 'I can't take this in,' she said. 'You can't spring this all on me, Malik. Not so suddenly, and then expect me to fall in with your plans without so much as a murmur.'

'I haven't suggested any plans.' But he would. Soon.

'I know, but...' Gracie sank her teeth into her lower lip again, and, despite the tension and anger and uncertainty, Malik felt his body respond, a sudden jolt of desire that appalled him. He couldn't feel even a shred of that for Gracie now. There was no point, and it would only cloud the issue at hand...securing the succession of the throne, and the stability of his country. 'Give me some time,' she implored. 'How about... How about we meet tomorrow? I could meet you at a restaurant...'

Malik gave her a long, hard look. She was trying to manage him. Him, the heir to the sultanate of Alazar, manipulated by a slip of a woman from Nowhereville, USA. His lip curled. 'Very well. I will arrange a place and send a car for you.'

'I can meet you...'

'It is not necessary. The car will come at seven o'clock.'

Irritation sparked in her eyes. She didn't like being managed, either. 'Seven-thirty.'

He almost smiled at that. 'Fine.' His gaze moved slowly over her, taking in the changes for the first time. Her hair was a shade darker than it had been ten years ago, although it still fell in tumbling curls and waves over her shoulders. Her body was still slender, although perhaps a little bit rounder, a little bit more womanly. Instead of youthful cut-offs and a T-shirt, she wore a khaki-coloured skirt and a summery cotton blouse dotted with tiny pink flowers. She still wore the kind of brightly coloured sneakers she'd had on in Rome, and the realisation almost made him smile again. She might be older, but Gracie Jones had not lost her spark. He was, bizarrely and pointlessly, glad of that.

Deliberately he moved his gaze back up to her face. 'Tomorrow night, then.' Malik turned to go. His hand was on the door when she spoke again.

'Malik…' Her voice was soft, and yet he stopped in his tracks. 'You haven't even asked his name.'

A new, unidentifiable emotion came at him like an arrow, piercing the steel he'd surrounded himself with for so long. His hand clenched on the doorknob, this strange new vulnerability unsettling him deeply. It was too much to process in that moment, too much to reveal. A lifetime of maintaining the armour of cold indifference could not be shed so quickly or easily. 'It doesn't matter,' he said shortly, the words wounding him as well as her, and then he opened the door and walked out.

Gracie didn't sleep at all that night. She lay in bed, the moonlight sifting silver patterns on the floor, as her mind raced and seethed, trying to make sense of Malik's bombshell of a visit.

Why did he want a father's rights to his son if he didn't even care about his name? What was really going on? Anxiety pulsed and writhed inside her as she thought of unleashing this new, frighteningly cold Malik on his son. He was, she feared, turning into his grandfather, a ruthless man interested only in the power he could wield. Or maybe he'd always been that way, and he'd just hidden it well. She didn't know him, she reminded herself. She'd *never* known him.

And she would not let Sam experience the same harsh cruelty she'd once felt from Malik—except she might not have any choice. Malik was Sam's father. As he'd said, he had rights. Rights Gracie might not be able to deny even if she wanted to.

The next morning, bleary-eyed and distracted, she snapped at Sam, who looked surprised and hurt before she pulled him in for a too-tight hug. She couldn't lose him. She wouldn't. In the middle of the night, in the darkness of her own frightened mind, she'd feared that Malik might spirit Sam away, snatch him on the way to school or even from his own bed. His horrible grandfather was certainly capable of it.

Now, however, with sunlight streaming through the window and the sound of children's laughter coming from outside, she wondered if she was being both paranoid and extreme. Surely Malik wouldn't commit a *crime*.

She still felt shaky inside that evening as she prepared to get ready for her dinner with Malik. She'd agonised over what to wear and had decided on business attire—a pair of tailored dark trousers and a crisp white blouse. She pulled her hair back with a clip and softened the look with a slick of lip gloss, adding red patent leather flats because sometimes it felt as if a splash of colour was her only reminder of how fun she'd used to be.

Her sister Anna knocked on the door to the apartment.

'Anybody home?' she called out before laughing as Sam barrelled into her. 'Hey, buddy. You ready to get going?'

'Yeah!' Sam crowed, and with a strained smile Gracie came into the kitchen.

'Thanks for having Sam tonight, Anna.'

'Any time, you know that. His cousins love sleepovers.' Anna had three young boys and they all adored Sam. Her sister glanced at her outfit, which was severe for her. 'Um…is this a job interview? For a funeral director? Because you don't normally dress like that.'

'Sort of,' Gracie admitted with a sigh. 'But not for a funeral director.' At least she hoped she wasn't sounding the death knell of life as she knew it.

Sam swung around to goggle at her. 'You're getting a new job? But I like you being at my school.'

'I'll still be at your school,' Gracie assured him. 'This is for something different.' Already she felt tangled up in a web of lies, but she wasn't ready to tell anyone about Malik or his visit.

Anna frowned at her. 'Are you okay? You seem tense.'

Gracie felt as if she might snap in half. 'I'm fine,' she assured her sister. 'Just a little nervous.'

Sam ran to get his stuff for the sleepover and Anna took a step closer to her, her eyes narrowed. 'Is this really a job interview?'

'Do I look like I dressed for a date?' Gracie tried to joke.

'I don't know.' Anna's frown deepened. 'Jonathan mentioned someone came to the house to see you last night. He said he looked scary.'

So that hadn't flown under the family's radar after all. 'He was just tall,' Gracie dismissed with a wobbly laugh. 'You know Jonathan.'

'Gracie…you haven't got yourself into some kind of… *trouble*, have you?'

Gracie glanced in the mirror and fussed with her hair, needing the distraction. 'What do you mean?'

'I don't know,' Anna confessed. 'With money or something…'

'Money?' Gracie turned from the mirror. 'Seriously? You think I had some loan shark coming around Mom and Dad's?'

Anna had the grace to look slightly abashed at this. 'I guess not.'

'I'm fine,' Gracie said with more conviction than she actually felt. 'Don't worry about me, Anna, please.' She was so tired of being the Jones kid who'd messed up and then made good, only sort of. She didn't want everyone clucking and sighing over her. She'd fix this. Somehow she'd fix this.

She waited outside on the pavement for the car Malik had said he would send, and then stared as a stretch limo came around the corner and pulled up in front of her parents' house. She saw curtains twitch at a dozen different windows and felt a surprised smile bloom across her face. Maybe Malik was trying to impress or intimidate, but she kind of liked the idea of the good people of Addison Heights seeing her being picked up in a limo.

Malik emerged from the car, looking devastatingly sexy in a black button-down shirt, open at the throat, and black trousers. His eyes gleamed in his face as he took in Gracie's appearance. Suddenly she wished she'd worn something feminine and flirty, but how stupid was that? She'd been seduced once by this man. She had no intention of succumbing again.

'I like the shoes,' Malik murmured, and Gracie blushed, those few words of simple flattery affecting her far too much.

'Thank you.'

Malik opened the door to the limo and Gracie slid inside, revelling in the soft leather seats, the unabashed luxury. There was a coffee table between the sofa-like seats, along with a huge bouquet of flowers.

'You could practically live in here,' she said as she noted the mini-fridge. 'All you need is a bed.' Immediately she wished she hadn't said that.

'And champagne,' Malik returned smoothly, magicking a bottle out of seemingly nowhere. Gracie stared at it, transfixed by the memory of another bottle of champagne, another lifetime.

'What are we celebrating?' she'd asked.

And he'd replied, *'Meeting.'*

'Why are you pulling out all the stops like this?' she asked after Malik had popped the cork and poured two foaming glasses of champagne. 'Last night you were Mr. Hard-Nosed and now…'

'I was shocked last night,' Malik admitted as he handed her a glass. 'So much of this has caught me by surprise. Discovering I had a son, seeing you again.' His gaze lingered on her for one sizzling moment before he looked away. 'I was not at my best. I apologise.'

The words sounded stilted, but the sentiment seemed sincere. *Maybe.* Surely she'd learned not to trust this man? 'Well.' She had no idea how to respond to any of it. 'Cheers.'

'Cheers,' Malik answered, and lifted his glass in a toast before taking a sip, his silvery gaze over the rim of the glass not leaving hers. Gracie had to force herself not to look away. She could feel her composure slipping, notch by notch. She'd wanted this meeting to be brisk and businesslike with her firmly in control, but a couple sips of champagne and she knew it was already spinning away from her.

'Where are we going to eat?' she asked. The limo was speeding down the road out of Addison Heights, which only offered a couple of diners and all-you-can-eat buffets. She couldn't picture Malik at either.

'Oriole, in Chicago.'

'What?' Gracie nearly dropped her champagne. 'That's an hour away.'

Malik's smile gleamed. 'I could not find a suitable place closer by.'

'And Oriole…' The name rang a bell. She'd read about it in a magazine, Chicago's newest and most exclusive Michelin-starred restaurant. 'How did you even get a reservation? I read that it's booked weeks and even months in advance.'

Malik gave a negligible shrug. 'Such things are not difficult.'

For a sultan. She finished the sentence herself silently. Despite the luxury and his obvious wealth, it was still hard to believe Malik was actually the heir to an entire country. That night in Rome he'd only been a boy, a wonderful boy she'd been head over heels for. The memory made her sad, somehow. Everything had changed.

She glanced out of the window at the road speeding by, the champagne sending pleasant bubbles zinging through her system. She felt weirdly tongue-tied, having no idea how to bridge the chasm of the last ten years. *How have you been?* seemed an absurd question at the moment.

'Tell me about our son,' Malik commanded in a low voice. Gracie tensed.

'Last night you didn't even want to know his name.'

'Peace, Grace. I already told you I wasn't at my best last night.'

And she hadn't been, either, spinning with shock from it all. She was still spinning. 'What do you want to know?'

'I do want to know his name,' Malik said, and she heard the barest hint of apology in his voice. She knew instinctively that she wouldn't get any more than that.

'It's Sam.'

Malik was silent, and Gracie turned from the window, risking another glance at his stern, autocratic profile. His mouth was compressed, his gaze shuttered. She had no idea what he was thinking.

'Sam,' he finally said. His voice sounded a little hoarse. 'It is a good name.'

'I'm glad you think so.' She was torn between gratitude and irritation, an unsettling mix. Just being with Malik was sending her emotions into a complete tailspin.

She took another sip of champagne, needing the distraction. Malik shifted in his seat, and Gracie was conscious of even that, the stretch of expensive fabric across his powerful thighs, the faint waft of exotic, citrusy cologne when he moved. More memories assailed her, sharp and sweet and so unbearably poignant.

For a second she could feel Malik's weight above her, his forearms braced by her head, his gaze intense and fiery as he'd moved inside her.

Prickly, shaming heat spread through her whole body. Why was she thinking this way, simply because of a whiff of cologne? But it was the same scent she remembered from a decade ago, and it flooded her senses.

'So,' she asked, her voice unnaturally loud and bright. 'How have you been?'

A faint smile flickered across Malik's face and was gone. 'Busy. How have you been, Grace?'

The question seemed loaded with some hidden meaning, as if he suspected she hadn't been all that well. He clearly hadn't been impressed by her apartment last night, and why should he have? Judging by this limo, Malik was used to unbelievable luxury.

'I've been fine,' she said firmly.

So that was pleasantries out of the way. Gracie's stomach swam with both nerves and champagne. She knew she should ask Malik what his intentions were, what he wanted for Sam, but she was too nervous to prod that sleeping dragon.

He leaned back in the seat, a relaxed and elegant sprawl, his finger and thumb braced against his temple. The gold and silver links of an expensive watch gleamed against one bronzed wrist. 'What have you been doing for the last ten years?'

'Besides raising our child?' she retorted, and then wished she hadn't. The word *our* suggested a reality that didn't exist. Except perhaps now it did.

'Besides that,' he agreed, unfazed by her sniping. 'Which of course is the most important job of all.'

'Of course,' she agreed, annoyed even by that. Malik no doubt had very traditional ideas about men's and women's roles. 'I stayed home with Sam while he was young. That cheque helped with that,' she added pointedly, but Malik remained unmoved. 'When Sam started school, I began working as a teaching assistant. I've been hoping to get certified for full-time teaching, maybe in special needs like I wanted to.' But she hadn't started yet because she hadn't saved up enough money for the course.

'And you've been living…' He trailed off, eyebrows raised expectantly.

'Above my parents' garage, yes,' Gracie finished with a touch of defensive ire. 'I like being near family and the price is right.' Why, she wondered, did she feel she had to defend herself?

'I'm glad you've had help,' Malik returned, and leaned forward to place a hand on her knee. Gracie felt as if she'd just deliberately stuck her finger in an electric socket. Her whole body jolted and she stared down at Malik's large brown hand, the fingers long and tapered, his palm seeming to burn through the fabric of her trousers. Did he realise how he was affecting her? Had that gesture been unthinking or calculated? *What did Malik want?*

With what felt like superhuman effort, Gracie pulled her leg away and angled her body towards the window. Her whole body still tingled from his touch. 'Thank you,' she muttered, and Malik just smiled.

'Tell me more about Sam,' he said after a moment, when Gracie's heart rate had finally started to slow. It kicked right up again. 'What is he like? Do you have a picture of him?'

'Yes...' With a weird mix of reluctance and anticipation, Gracie dug her phone out of her bag and scrolled through the photos, looking for a decent one of Sam. Most of them were of him in various states of activity, laughter and exuberance. She found a decent one of him head-on and silently handed the phone to Malik. Their fingers brushed as he took it and she tried to quell the frisson of awareness that went through her at that tiny touch. Ten years and he affected her just as he ever had, maybe even more.

Malik stared down at the phone, his expression impassive. Gracie's heart lurched. What was he thinking as he looked at a picture of their son? Did he notice how Sam had his silvery eyes but her gap-toothed smile, at least the one she'd had as a child? But he wouldn't know that, of course. There was so much he didn't know about her, just as there was so much she didn't know about him. They were strangers, bound by the beautiful and precious human being whose image Malik held in his hand.

Silently he started to hand the phone back to her, but his thumb slipped on the screen and the photos started to scroll forward. Another image of Sam appeared, this one of him goofing around in the kitchen, a silly expression on his face. Malik froze and then glanced at Gracie from under thick, dark lashes, his expression still shuttered.

'May I?' he asked, gesturing to the phone. Wordlessly she nodded and then sat there, her breath held, as Malik scrolled through the photos without speaking.

Sam grinning at the camera, Sam hamming it up in the backyard with some friends, Sam proudly holding third-place prize in the school spelling bee. Malik glanced at each photo for a few silent seconds before swiping to the next one. They were all, Gracie realised, pictures of Sam. And still he didn't say a word.

Questions bubbled to her lips and she forced them down.

She wasn't going to ask Malik what he thought. She wasn't going to beg for him to give some sign of what he was feeling, some word of praise or approval for the son he now claimed he wanted to know. Although, Gracie realised, he hadn't actually claimed any such thing. Malik hadn't told her one word about why he'd burst so suddenly into their lives, simply that he'd discovered Sam's existence.

They didn't talk until the limo pulled up to the restaurant in Chicago's West Loop neighbourhood. As Gracie stepped out of the car, Malik rested one hand on the small of her back; she could feel the warm, insistent press of his palm and didn't know whether to ignore it or lean into the caress.

The black-jacketed maître d' opened the door himself and ushered them into an elegant restaurant that was lit by candles and completely empty.

Gracie turned to Malik in surprise. 'I thought this place was booked months in advance...'

'I took the liberty of hiring the entire restaurant,' Malik replied with a shrug. 'I wanted to ensure our privacy.'

'Your Highness,' the maître d' murmured. 'We are so pleased to have you visit us.'

Gracie had to keep her jaw from dropping as they were ushered to the single table set apart from the others, awash with candlelight and laden with crystal. She sat down, her mind still spinning, as Malik sat across from her and the sommelier handed him the extensive wine list.

'You reserved the whole restaurant?' she said, still disbelieving, her voice lowered to a whisper.

Malik raised his eyebrows as he looked up from the wine list. 'Yes, what of it?'

'It's just...this place is being written up in all the magazines. People, even famous and rich people, wait months for a reservation.'

A small smile played about Malik's mouth. 'And?'

And with that single word Gracie realised afresh how powerful Malik was. The Sultan-in-Waiting of Alazar. A shiver of apprehension rippled through her.

'Why didn't you tell me you were the heir to the throne?' she asked. 'Back then?'

Awareness and memory flared in Malik's iron-grey eyes and too late Gracie realised she shouldn't have referenced *back then*. That one magical, amazing, terrible night.

'I wanted to keep a low profile.'

She decided to salvage her wounded pride by saying, 'I would have thought your title would have added to your appeal.'

Black brows snapped together dangerously. 'What do you mean?'

A shrug, to show how little it mattered now. 'Only that it's a good chat-up line, isn't it? Not that you needed a chat-up line with me. I practically fell into your arms.' The memory of how quickly and eagerly she'd bought the whole connection spiel brought a flush of shame to her face. She lowered her head, letting her hair swing down, to hide her expression.

Malik looked as if he wanted to disagree, but he merely pressed his lips together as he scanned the menu. 'That was then, this is now.'

'Very true.' And *now* was going to be a whole lot of different.

'The past doesn't matter any more, except in relation to Sam.'

Which was her cue to ask what his intentions were. But before she could summon the courage to so much as open her mouth, a waiter materialised by Malik's elbow. 'Your Highness would like to order?'

'Yes, I'll start with the langoustine and Miss Jones will have the oysters on the half shell.'

'Very good.'

Gracie listened, open-mouthed, as Malik ordered her entire meal without consulting her once. He handed the menu to the waiter and, with a pointed look he completely ignored, Gracie handed hers over, as well.

'I obviously didn't need that.'

Malik looked nonplussed. 'Need what?'

'The menu. Since you were going to order for me.' She didn't bother to keep the pique out of her voice. 'What if I don't like oysters?'

'Have you had them before?'

And now she was caught out. 'No,' Gracie said after a moment, 'but that's not the point.'

'Isn't it? I'd like you to have new experiences, Grace. Adventures. Isn't that what you once wanted?'

Gracie took a few scattered seconds to formulate her reply. 'I'd like to choose my own adventures, thank you very much.'

'I'll keep that in mind,' Malik said in a tone that suggested he would do no such thing. And what adventures was he even talking about? What kind of future was he referring to?

'Malik…' Gracie licked her lips, her mouth turning dry. Just saying his name made her feel strange. Made her remember. 'Why have you come here? What…what do you want with Sam?' She released a low breath, relief and trepidation warring within her. At least it was out there now. He had to answer, surely.

But Malik didn't speak for a long moment. His eyes were fathomless and opaque, like pools of silver ice, glacial lakes. His mouth pursed and then relaxed as he sat back in his chair, one hand toying with the stem of his empty wine glass. 'It is natural, is it not, to want to meet your own child? Until three days ago, I had no idea I had a son. Of course I would come.'

Not necessarily, Gracie wanted to say but didn't quite dare. Not considering how his grandfather had reacted, or how Malik had pushed her away that wretched morning after. 'So...' Gracie began carefully, 'you want to meet Sam?'

'Of course.'

'And then...?' As she held her breath, she realised she didn't know what she was hoping for. For Malik to say he'd return to Alazar and leave them alone? But Sam would be crushed to meet his father and then have him disappear. And yet...what was the alternative? For Malik to be a part of their lives? The thought of him setting up some kind of house or life in Addison Heights was absurd.

Her mind spun in circles, coming up against dead ends at every turn. *What did Malik want?*

'And then,' Malik said, his voice as calm and unruffled as a summer sea, 'you and Sam will come with me to Alazar.'

CHAPTER FIVE

HE HAD TO PLAY this very carefully. Malik watched as Gracie's lovely eyes widened and her jaw dropped. For a few seconds she didn't speak. The sommelier took the opportunity to come forward with the very expensive bottle of wine Malik had ordered. He poured a generous mouthful into Malik's glass and Malik drank, his eyes on Gracie as she snapped her mouth closed and stared at him, flummoxed and fuming.

'Very good,' Malik said, dismissing the sommelier. The other staff retreated to a discreet distance. Gracie leaned forward, her hazel eyes glinting with both shock and outrage.

'We can't just come to *Alazar*.'

Malik bit back the autocratic retorts that sprang so quickly to his lips. Since hearing about his son he'd wanted to do nothing more than drag Gracie and Sam onto the royal jet as quickly as possible and get them back to Alazar, safe and secure. He'd been tempted more than once since coming to America to do just that, and damn Gracie's finer feelings. Fortunately he'd learned both restraint and discretion in ten years of managing warring Bedouin tribes. He needed to play a long game now, and for the moment, at least, he needed Gracie's cooperation.

'Why not?' he asked.

Gracie's fair eyebrows rose. 'Why not?' she repeated, as if she could scarcely believe the question.

Malik nodded. 'Yes. Why not?'

It was a simple question, and yet still she boggled. 'Because…because he has school and I have a job and friends and a life…and we just can't.'

She was afraid. Malik saw it in her eyes and the way her hands clenched on the tabletop before she hid them in her lap. But what exactly was Gracie afraid of? Did she suspect what he intended? She must, at least a little. Surely she had to realise the life she'd been living no longer existed. Nothing could be the same for her ever again. Judging from what he'd seen of her life so far, that was not necessarily a bad thing.

'I think you can,' Malik said smoothly. He kept his voice low, pleasant and mild. He felt almost as if he were taming one of the Bedouin's wild Arabians. The halter he would slip on later, when it was too late for her to bolt. 'It is almost the summer holiday, is it not?'

'Yes…'

'So Sam will be out of school and you will be free from work.' She said nothing, and he continued, deliberately gentling his voice, 'Why not have a two-week holiday? Give Sam the opportunity to discover his roots and get to know his father?' A tremor went through him at that thought, but he masked it. 'Surely that is a reasonable request, Grace.'

She gazed down into her wine, clearly battling against the idea. 'What happens after that?' she asked in a low voice. 'You can't just breeze in and out of Sam's life.'

'I have no intention of doing that,' Malik returned evenly. *No intention at all.* He paused, not wanting to lie to her face and yet knowing she could in no way handle the truth at this point. 'I intend to be part of Sam's life from now on. How that manifests itself remains to be seen and is subject to both of our agreement, of course.'

Relief flickered through her eyes, followed by dawning fear. 'You mean...a custody arrangement?'

Malik spread his hands. 'Let us use these next two weeks to decide together the best way forward.' He paused for only a moment before continuing, 'This could be enjoyable for all of us, Grace. An adventure, yes? A chance to show Sam some of the world and to experience it yourself. Why resist?'

Why resist? It felt like a siren song, but it was also starting to sound sensible. A two-week luxury holiday was certainly something Sam hadn't experienced, and Malik was right. Both he and Sam needed a chance to get to know each other. Yet Gracie still resisted instinctively, out of fear. Fear for her son but also fear for herself. She had not been able to resist this man once before. She was afraid she might not resist him again...and now so much more was at stake. Her son. Her *life*.

But...two weeks. It wasn't a lifetime, and she liked the thought of showing her family and neighbours that she wasn't quite the screw-up they all silently seemed to think she was. Instead of being a struggling single mom, she had a glamorous and important man arrive to sweep both her and Sam away, at least for a little while. Was she shallow to care about that? Did it make her weak?

In that moment she didn't care. Malik was waiting for her response, his silvery gaze resting intently on her, and his reasons made sense.

'All right,' she said, and released the breath she hadn't realised she was holding. 'We'll come for two weeks.'

Malik's answering smile broke over her like a wave, left her dazed and reeling. He was irresistible when he smiled.

His eyes lightened and he reminded her of who he'd used to be. Who she'd once thought he was. Dangerous, that smile. She'd have to develop an immunity to it.

'Thank you, Grace,' Malik said, and he leaned over and squeezed her hand. That was dangerous, too, the slide of his fingers over hers making Gracie want to shiver. *Tremble.* More memories tumbled through her mind, a sensual kaleidoscope she had to suppress. She couldn't survive two weeks with Malik al Bahjat if he was going to turn on the charm.

'When would you like us to go?' she asked, determined to recapture a little of the brisk practicality she'd been hoping to have for this meeting.

'Tomorrow.'

'What?' So much for that. 'We can't go tomorrow, Malik. Sam doesn't even have a passport.'

'That can be arranged.'

Gracie shook her head, unsure whether to be impressed or terrified by the extent of Malik's power. She was both. 'Why do we have to move so fast? And what am I to tell Sam? And my family—'

'The truth.' For a second an edge of iron entered Malik's voice, reminding Gracie just who she was dealing with. He could turn on the charm, and he could just as easily and quickly turn it off.

'Which is?' she demanded, refusing to be cowed. 'Do I tell Sam you're his father?'

'I'll tell him,' Malik stated. 'When the time is right. And why not tell your parents you've been swept away by a sheikh for the holiday of a lifetime?'

He smiled again, and she was not immune. Not yet, anyway. 'So not the truth, then.'

'A version of it, at least.'

'Some version.' She shook her head, sensing how futile it was to resist Malik's will and yet needing to try anyway, for her own sake. 'You're being unreasonable. I have to give notice at school—there's still a week left. And Sam, as well...'

'Like I said, it can be arranged. I am the leader of a country, Grace. I cannot wait around here while Sam finishes a couple days of school.' Their first course arrived with a flourish, and Gracie glanced down at the oysters lying in their shells on a bed of crushed ice.

She glanced at Malik's plate of langoustines and did not know which dish looked more awkward to eat. 'Well, this is an adventure,' she said with a touch of acerbity, and Malik laughed, a rich, full-bodied sound that had her blinking in surprise. She'd never heard him laugh like that.

'I think you'll like them,' he said. 'Do you know how to eat them?'

'There's a method?'

'Only if you don't want to get them all over yourself.' He leaned across, taking the tiny fork that had been left with the plate and freeing an oyster from its shell. Gracie expected him to sit back, but instead he took the oyster in his hand and lifted it to her lips. She jerked back in surprise.

'What...?'

'You just slurp it down,' he said, his voice low and sensual. His eyes, hot and heavy-lidded, were on her. Gracie felt entirely discomfited.

'Slurp it,' she repeated, unconvinced. She did not think she would look particularly attractive slurping raw fish from Malik's hand. But why did she care about looking attractive?

'Go ahead, Grace,' Malik murmured. 'I think you'll like it.' Was she imagining the suggestive note in his voice, the hint of humour, the promise of sensuality? Why was he doing this? He had to be toying with her. The realisation both annoyed and hurt and in one gulp she took the oyster in her mouth and it slithered down her throat.

'Delicious?' Malik prompted, and Gracie tried not to make a face. She wasn't as adventurous as all that, apparently. 'They're an aphrodisiac, you know.'

'So I've heard,' Gracie returned tartly. 'I remain unconvinced.'

'You need convincing?'

Her heart lurched, tangling with her ribs. 'Don't, Malik,' she said quietly, not daring to say more, and Malik sat back, watching her with a thoughtful, assessing gaze.

For lack of anything else to do she ate another oyster on her own. Malik took one of his langoustines and cracked it open in one swift movement, neatly extracting the tail meat.

'I think you've lived a very quiet life for the last ten years,' he said.

'If you mean I haven't gone to places like this and eaten oysters, then you'd be right,' Gracie retorted, stung.

'It wasn't meant to be a criticism.'

'Funny, it felt like one. I've liked my life fine, you know, but obviously I still seem like a country bumpkin to you.' She heard the throb of hurt in her voice and closed her eyes. *Why* had she said that?

'Grace.' Malik's voice was like a caress. 'I never thought of you like that.'

'It doesn't matter.' She plucked another oyster and popped it into her mouth. She was almost starting to like these suckers. 'As you said before, that was the past, and this is the present. The last thing either of us needs to do now is a postmortem on that ill-conceived night a million years ago.'

Malik tilted his head. 'Ill-conceived?' he repeated softly, and Gracie flushed.

'Of course I didn't mean it like *that*. Sam is the best thing that ever happened to me.'

'And to me,' Malik said with such heartfelt sincerity that Gracie was left blinking, her mouth opening and closing without a word coming out.

'But you don't even know him,' she managed.

'I will remedy that situation tomorrow,' Malik returned. 'Happily.'

'And who do I tell him you are?' Gracie asked. 'How do I explain this huge holiday?'

'Do ten-year-old boys need explanations for holidays?' Malik asked with a whimsical lift of his brows. 'I doubt he will question it.'

Gracie acknowledged this truth silently. Sam would be thrilled to go on holiday. He certainly wouldn't care how or why it came to pass. Maybe she really needed to let go of her resistance. Because it was her resistance, not Sam's. She was afraid of Malik. Afraid of being tempted. *Hurt.* And that simply wasn't a good enough reason to dig in her heels.

She knew then that she could not deny her son his heritage or his birthright simply because of her own nervousness—and attraction.

'Very well,' she said, and tried to ignore the shiver of apprehension—and excitement—that went through her at the simple fact of her acquiescence.

'Good. I will arrange for you and Sam to be picked up tomorrow morning.'

'Where will you be?'

'I have business to see to, but I will meet you at the airstrip, on the royal jet.'

The royal jet. Could things get any more fantastic? Gracie swallowed dryly. She could hardly believe she was agreeing to this, and yet she felt a quiver of excitement low in her belly…and wondered just exactly what she was excited about. 'Very well,' she said again, and Malik subjected her to another brilliant smile.

'You have convinced her?' Asad demanded. Malik gazed at his grandfather's face on the screen of his laptop and tried to ignore the churning mixture of guilt and anticipation that had soured his gut since he'd left Gracie two hours before.

She'd looked so unsure, fragile and hopeful at the same time. As she'd slipped out of the limo, one slender hand on the door, Malik had fought the urge to take her in his arms and kiss her. In that moment he had remembered exactly how soft her lips had felt, and how sweet she'd tasted. And he'd wanted to reacquaint himself with both sensations.

'See you tomorrow?' she'd said, a questioning lilt in her voice, as if she could scarcely believe she was really going with him.

'Tomorrow,' Malik had promised, and he'd waited until she'd gone into her flat before he'd ordered the driver to start the journey back to his five-star hotel in Chicago.

'Yes.' Malik's reply was terse. He'd convinced Gracie to come to Alazar, but there was so much she still didn't know—that Sam was his heir, that Sam's place and her own had to be in his country. That they would marry. Considering how much resistance she'd put up to a two-week visit, Malik could only imagine her reaction when he told her of his true intentions.

And yet…he'd seen excitement in Gracie's eyes. Desire, too. She remembered how it had been between them. And he believed she was eager for new experiences, perhaps even a new life. Convincing her of all the advantages would be a challenge, but one he was capable of rising to. He had to be.

'You will marry as soon as you arrive,' Asad stated, and Malik forced the irritation from his voice as he answered levelly.

'We will marry when I decree the time is right.'

'Sam must be legitimised as soon as possible—'

'I know.' Realistically Malik knew he could enforce his will as soon as Gracie was on the royal jet. She'd have few alternatives other than to do as he commanded, and yet he resisted that roughshod approach. It would only embitter Gracie, and perhaps Sam, as well. Time was of the essence, but he hoped he could accomplish what he needed to in a gentler manner. Not, he acknowledged, that he even knew how to be gentle.

Playing soft with Gracie tonight had been an exercise in dramatics, and yet he'd found he'd meant some of it. He'd certainly enjoyed those brief touches, and the light flirting. Watching her eat oysters had been an exquisite torture.

'In any case,' he told Asad, 'I must end the engagement to Johara before I marry another. That will be a delicate matter.'

'True.' A cough racked Asad's body. 'Still, you must work quickly. Any whispers of instability…'

'I know.' The country's peace was still a new and untested thing. The sooner Malik was married with an heir in place, the better. 'Leave it to me, Grandfather. I can manage it.'

With a terse farewell Malik disconnected the video call. Staring out at the lights of the city, he realised he could not ease his regret and uncertainty. He didn't like deceiving Gracie, and yet he knew he had no choice. Alazar had to come first.

Restlessly Malik rose from his seat and paced the elegant confines of his penthouse suite. He didn't like being reminded of the boy he'd once been. He'd been so innocent at twenty-two, so woefully inexperienced in every way. His life had been about training and waiting, and then he'd been catapulted into the harsh realities of adulthood when Alazar had been plunged into near civil war.

Being with Gracie tonight had brought him back to that boy. Made him feel hope and desire and something deeper than either, and that was dangerous. He needed Gracie, yes, but only as a matter of expediency. He had no intention of feeling anything for her, of giving in to emotion or, worse, love. Those feelings were signs of weakness and led to destruction. His father had certainly shown him that. Malik could still remember the look of utter despair on his father's face, the sobs that had continually racked his body. The shell of a person he'd become. All he intended to feel for Gracie, he assured himself, was simple sexual desire—and that would soon be sated. Nothing else would ever be up for discussion.

'Mom?' Sam looked up from his bowl of cereal, his dark eyebrows raised.

He looked like Malik, something that had always been impossible to ignore even though Gracie had certainly tried. Floppy dark hair, bronzed skin, a tall, rangy build, a sense of confidence and ability that was innate. Yes, Sam was most certainly Malik's son. A son of Alazar.

'Are you okay?'

'Yes.' Gracie took a deep breath and tried for a smile. 'Actually, I need to talk to you.'

It was eight o'clock on Friday morning and Sam was dressed for school. How on earth could she explain to him that instead he would be getting on a plane and travelling to a country he'd probably never heard of…with his father? But, no. The last part was for Malik to tell.

'What is it?' Sam asked, sensing her hesitation.

'How…how would you like to go on a holiday? An amazing holiday?'

Sam's eyebrows drew together in a way that was eerily reminiscent of Malik. 'Is this a trick question?'

'No.'

'What kind of amazing holiday?'

'To a place called Alazar.'

'Alazar!' Sam's face brightened. 'It has the highest mountain in the Middle East.'

'Does it?' Gracie smiled and shook her head. Of course her son had heard of Alazar and knew some obscure geographical fact about it. Of course he was going to be wildly excited about going. 'Well, how would you like to visit there?'

'Really?' Sam's eyes rounded as he bounced in his chair. 'Just like that? When do we go?'

'Um…today.'

'Today!' Sam stared at her in grinning disbelief and then bounced again, harder this time, so Gracie had to fling out one hand to keep the chair's balance. 'That is *awesome*. When do we leave?'

'A car is coming for us around lunchtime.'

'So we need to pack!' Sam rose from his chair. 'How much stuff should I bring?'

She had no idea. Would he need formal clothes? What would they be doing for two whole weeks? Swallowing down the butterflies that threatened to overwhelm her, Gracie rose from her chair and poured herself a much-needed second cup of coffee. 'A little bit of everything, I guess. I don't actually know anything about Alazar.' Except its Sultan. 'I suppose it will be pretty hot.'

Sam, halfway to his bedroom, stopped and turned around. 'Why are we going there?' he asked, and Gracie couldn't tell if he was suspicious or just interested. 'If you didn't know anything about it?'

'Well.' Gracie took a sip of coffee to stall for time. She'd stayed up until the small hours of the morning thinking about how to explain this to Sam—as well as reliving every moment she'd spent with Malik. 'I have a friend who is in the government there, and he's invited us to stay.'

'Really?' Sam goggled at her. 'How did you meet someone like that?'

'I met him a long time ago, during my travels in Europe.'

'Wow. So cool. I can't wait to tell everyone at school!'

'Yes, but you'll miss the last week of school, Sam—'

'Oh, who cares.' Sam dismissed with a shrug. 'We never do anything then anyway.' And then, whistling, he disappeared into his bedroom. Gracie sank into her chair, clutching her coffee cup. That had been remarkably easy, just as Malik had predicted. And yet there was still so much that was unknown, so many hurdles to jump. But one step at a time, she told herself. One inch at a time if necessary. She didn't think she could handle any more.

CHAPTER SIX

'GOODNESS.'

Gracie shaded her eyes from the glare of the sunlight with one hand as she glanced up at the royal jet of Alazar, a gleaming black machine with wavy red stripes on the tail and wings. Next to her Sam let out a low hiss of breath, a sound of awe and excitement.

All morning he'd been running around the apartment like a mad thing, jumping on the bed and the sofa while Gracie had thrown things in suitcases and wondered what on earth she was supposed to wear. Would they be staying at some palace? Would there be formal occasions? Or would it all be casual, hanging out by a pool and reading paperbacks? She had no idea about any of it, what to expect from the trip—and from Malik.

That morning she'd had the most awkward and bizarre conversation of her life with her parents, explaining who Sam's father was and why they were now going to Alazar.

'A sultan?' Her father's eyes had boggled. 'Gracie, are you sure he's not having you on?'

Gracie had almost laughed at that. Poor, stupid Gracie who had managed not just to get herself knocked up but duped, too, by some con man. She knew her father meant it well, but she was tired of the scepticism and doubt.

'I'm quite sure, Dad,' she'd replied a bit sharply. She

had no doubt about who Malik was in that respect. She simply didn't know who he was any more as a person, as a man—if she'd ever known.

But now she was going to find out. At least for two weeks.

'We're going on that plane?' Sam asked in an awed voice. 'That is *awesome*.'

'I'm glad you think so.'

As they stood in front of the jet, Malik emerged from its interior, dressed in grey trousers and a button-down shirt open at the throat. His hair was swept back from his face, his eyes dark and fathomless under the slashes of his eyebrows, his mouth unsmiling as he came down the stairs towards them. Sam inched closer to Gracie.

'Who is that…?' he whispered. He sounded a little fearful.

'That's…' The word stuck in her throat. Why did Malik have to look so ferocious? Where was that smile now? 'That's my friend.'

'Hello, Sam.' Malik came to stand before Sam, his mouth betraying not even a hint of a smile, his gaze intent and serious.

Sam looked up at him nervously. 'How do you know my name?'

'Your mother told me.' Malik was silent for a moment, his gaze searching Sam's face. 'I'm very pleased to meet you.'

'Okay.' Sam glanced at his mother uncertainly. 'Is this your plane?'

'Yes.'

'Wow.'

'Would you like to see it?'

Sam's eyes lit up and his uncertainty fell away. 'Yeah!'

The tension that had been knotting Gracie's shoulder

blades eased a little bit as they walked up the steps into the plane. The inside of the jet was a study in unfettered luxury, and Sam's mouth wasn't the only one dropping open.

He exclaimed over the deep leather sofas, the velvet throw pillows and glass coffee tables, the bowls of exotic fruit and nuts scattered around. Gracie felt as if she were in a five-star hotel suite.

'Wow.' She managed a smile for Malik. 'This is amazing.'

'It is yours to enjoy.' Malik gestured to one of the sofas. 'Please, make yourself comfortable. Whatever you wish for, one of the stewards will be happy to provide.'

'Anything?' Sam's eyes had gone ridiculously round. In addition to two white-jacketed stewards waiting attentively with silver trays and glasses of champagne, Gracie noticed the burly security guards who stood by the now closed door. A feeling of claustrophobia clawed at her insides and she forced it away. Of course there would be guards.

'Relax,' Malik murmured, and he placed one hand on her arm. The feel of his fingers on her skin sent an electrical charge skittering along her nerve endings. 'You're safe, Grace.'

'This feels a little bit like a gilded prison,' she returned lightly. Sam was busy exploring the interior of the plane and couldn't hear her. 'I suppose you get used to being surrounded by guards.'

'It is, unfortunately, a necessity.'

A new thought struck her. 'We're not... Sam's not in danger, is he? I mean, Alazar is a safe place?' Why hadn't she done an Internet search on it last night?

'You will be completely safe at all times.' Malik hesitated, and Gracie knew there was something else.

'What?' she demanded. 'What are you not telling me?'

'There has been some instability in the more remote regions of my country. Bedouin tribes warring as well as wishing for things to be more traditional. But it is peaceful now.'

'Now? But it wasn't?'

'It will not concern you or Sam,' Malik said smoothly. 'I, along with my government, have worked hard these last few years to keep my country peaceful and help it to become modern.'

'Oh.' That all sounded rather important. 'What kinds of things do you mean?'

He shrugged. 'Developing a national healthcare system, increasing opportunities for education, trade agreements with the West. Some of the tribes do not like or want these things, but the people in the cities, such as the capital, Teruk, do. It is a balancing act.' He took a step towards her, lowering his voice so Sam couldn't overhear. 'I look forward to showing both you and Sam my country. It is his heritage, after all. But I promise you, you will be safe at all times. That will be my highest priority.' His gaze rested on hers, blazing with intent, and Gracie nodded, reassured.

'Thank you.' Maybe she needed to relax a little. Gracie let out the breath she hadn't realised she was holding. She was in the middle of the most incredibly luxurious surroundings she'd ever been in. Maybe she needed to start enjoying the adventure Malik had given her, instead of assuming the worst.

'Why don't you come and explore the plane?' Malik suggested. 'We have a few moments before takeoff.'

'Okay.' Gracie nodded towards Sam, who was exploring the far side of the cabin. 'When are you going to...?'

'Soon.' Malik rested his hand on her arm once more, and the same shivers raced through her body. Would she ever stop reacting to his touch? 'Let's get to know each other first. Relax a little bit.'

It made sense, even if she still felt keyed up. 'All right.'

Malik felt as if he couldn't trust the expression on his face as he walked behind Gracie and Sam. He felt an odd and unsettling mixture of elation and regret, both of them intense in the way they assailed him. He had just met his *son*. His son. Who looked just like him. Who seemed inquisitive and interesting and bright. Who seemed to accept all of this and, most important, *him* in one generous swoop of easy affection. Yet how would Sam react to the news that he was his father? The prospect of telling Sam the truth made Malik feel both overjoyed and afraid. After years of numbness, the emotion was almost too much to bear.

He caught Gracie frowning at him slightly, a look of concern in her eyes. Malik tried to smile, but his face felt stiff. His relaxed manner was nothing more than a façade, an act, because inside he felt as if he wanted to whoop or weep or both. He hadn't expected to feel this rush of emotion, maybe even love, for a boy he'd never even seen before. The biological bonds were stronger than he'd expected. The role of father felt both strange and natural.

He felt the light touch of a hand on his, and he looked down to see Gracie squeezing his fingers, a tiny caress of support and understanding that affected him far too much. He managed a smile and with a small smile back she removed her hand. As soon as it was gone Malik missed it.

'Wow,' Sam exclaimed as they came into the media room. 'That's the biggest TV I've ever seen.' He was soon asking Malik questions about everything, from how the satellite television worked to whether the plane adhered to international safety standards.

'I believe it does,' Malik answered solemnly before

catching Gracie's smiling gaze over Sam's head. Suddenly he felt warm all over, not with simple lust for the woman whose touch he still remembered, but with *happiness*. It was such an unaccustomed feeling that it took him a moment to recognise it. He was enjoying himself. He hadn't enjoyed himself this much in ten years...since he'd last been with Gracie.

'He's like this all the time,' Gracie confided as Sam raced ahead to explore the next part of the jet. 'Asking questions about everything.'

'That is a good thing,' Malik answered. 'You have raised him well.'

Startled, Gracie glanced at him, a flush creeping over her face. 'Well, thank you.'

'You sound surprised.'

'I suppose I'm not used to compliments.'

Malik frowned. 'Why not?'

'Well... I'm sort of known as "the Jones screw-up" back home.' As if she felt she'd admitted too much, she let out a slightly forced laugh and looked away. 'More of a joke than anything else, really, but it can still sting.'

Malik laid a staying hand on her arm. 'Why would you be known as that?' He realised he hated the idea of anyone putting Gracie down.

Sam was out of earshot in the small library. Malik waited, wanting to hear her confidence, to gain her trust, even if he hadn't earned it yet. Even if he didn't deserve it, considering how little he'd told her of his true plans.

'It's just that in a small town like Addison Heights, my situation was seen as...unfortunate,' Gracie said at last.

'Your situation?'

Wry exasperation lit her eyes as she looked up at him. 'Malik, I came home from a backpacking trip through Europe pregnant with a stranger's baby. I dropped out of university before I even had a chance to begin and have been scraping a living together ever since, while living above my parents' garage. Yes, I'm seen as a screw-up. Not,' she added fiercely, shaking off his arm, 'that I regret anything. And I like my life. I like my job. I know you look down on it, but I wouldn't change a bit of it. Sam is worth everything.'

'Of course he is,' Malik murmured. He felt a strange mixture of gratification and sadness for Gracie, for the little life she'd managed, through sheer strength of will and determination, to carve out for herself. But the mercenary part of him acknowledged that it would, perhaps, not be so difficult for her to leave it. 'I'm sorry.'

'None of it's your fault. Well, besides the genes.' She slid him a rueful smile. 'Sam didn't get his stubbornness or chronic ear infections from me.'

'I might have contributed to those traits,' Malik answered with a smile. 'I was a rather sickly child.'

'Good thing he looks like he'll grow out of it,' Gracie quipped. 'I certainly wouldn't call you sickly now.'

Her eyes dropped from his face and she did a quick once-over of his body that left Malik with a searing heat blazing through him. Gracie must have felt it, too, for her cheeks went pink and she looked away.

Desire swirled through his veins, a molten need he struggled to suppress. His attraction to Gracie was just as strong as it ever was, if not even stronger. Enforced celibacy during his time in the desert hadn't helped.

Malik considered the matter as he and Gracie followed Sam to the library. Sex could complicate things, of course, especially for a woman, but if he and Gracie were to marry, they would have a normal union in that regard. He certainly didn't intend to be celibate. A healthy, passionate marriage based on the bedrock of a shared child. It made sense...to him. And he would make sure it made sense to Gracie.

They spent a pleasant few minutes exploring the rest of the jet's luxuries, ending up in the bedroom in the back with its sumptuous en-suite bathroom. Gracie glanced at the king-sized bed with its cream satin sheets and Malik saw a faint blush touch her cheeks once more. The desire that had quieted within him rose to a roar again.

Was she remembering that night in all of its exquisite detail? He was. Even now, ten years later, he could recall every poignant, pleasurable second of their night together, if he let himself. Right now he was dangerously tempted to indulge every sensual, perfect memory.

He turned away from the bed. 'We should sit down for takeoff,' he said. 'But once we're in the air, you can move around as you like. I'm sure there's plenty you'd still like to see, Sam.'

'This really is amazing,' Gracie murmured. 'Thank you.'

'It is my pleasure.'

They took their seats in the main cabin of the plane. Sam sat by the window, his nose pressed to the glass as he scoured the airfield, eager for the next phase of this adventure to begin.

'He's never been on an airplane before,' Gracie explained with a small smile. 'He's been bouncing around all day, wild with excitement.'

'There will be many firsts on this trip,' Malik answered. 'I hope he enjoys them all with the same vigour.'

'I'm sure he will.' Gracie looked away, giving him the opportunity to study her. She was as beautiful and as vibrant as ever, even though she looked a little strained. The curve of her cheek, the sweep of her hair all felt familiar to him, and his palms itched with the memory of how they had once traced those curves and dips, learned them by heart.

He knew he had to stop letting those sweet memories affect him so much. Their power was a danger to him, and always had been. He could not allow himself to be torn in two by the needs of his country and the wants of his body. Duty and desire. Desire could perhaps be gratified, but duty always had to win.

'We're taking off!' Sam exclaimed, and Gracie gave Malik a wry look that he returned, a smile tipping the corners of her mouth and buoying his heart. He'd forgotten how much Gracie made him smile, how she *lightened* him. She looked away quickly, and he knew she was as unsettled as he was by the spark that still existed between them, the bonds of remembrance stronger than either of them had anticipated. The past called to them both, a siren song Malik would make the most of.

He leaned forward, touching her knee lightly, noting and enjoying the way her body tensed beneath his hand. 'He is a wonderful boy.'

Startled, she jerked back to look at him, her lips slightly parted, her eyes wide. 'You can say that, after just a few minutes?'

'Yes.' He spoke solemnly, firmly and with utter conviction. She gave a short, breathy laugh.

'Well, thank you, I guess. I don't know how much of that is up to me.' His hand was still on her knee, and he was loath to remove it. The warmth of her skin burned into his palm, his soul. He felt more alive now than he had in years.

Gracie glanced at Sam, who still had his nose pressed to the window, his hair flopping over his eyes. He pushed it back with an impatient hand.

'He could fall in love with you,' she said in a low voice.

'With all of this.' Her gaze was downcast, her lashes sweeping her cheeks. 'When you tell him...I know he'll be thrilled. It's like a fairy tale come true, isn't it? Your missing father turns out to be a king.' Her voice trembled and so did her lips. She pressed them together. 'Don't break his heart, Malik, please.'

Malik felt as if his own heart had just suffered a serious knock. He didn't deserve even the possibility of his son's unstinting, easy affection. He didn't know what to do with love. 'I won't,' he said, his voice a rasp, even as he acknowledged to himself this was a promise he had no idea if he could keep.

Gracie shifted her legs and he let his hand fall away. 'You'd better not,' she whispered, and blinked back tears.

Malik sat back in his seat and Gracie kept her face averted, trying desperately to hold on to her composure. She'd known this would be difficult, but she hadn't expected to feel so *raw*. So vulnerable, and in so many ways. Seeing Sam with Malik even so briefly had opened up a need inside her that she hadn't let herself ever acknowledge. A need for Sam to have a father, for her to have an ally. A partner.

And you actually think that's Malik?

The prospect was so ludicrous she would have laughed. All they'd had was a one-night stand. Yes, she'd seen glimpses of the old Malik, the fake Malik, or so she'd thought, today. When he stopped being so stern and autocratic, he could be gentle and funny and kind.

No. She couldn't think like that. She was here for two weeks, and after that they'd come to some sort of custody arrangement. Gracie hadn't dared to think that far ahead, but now she forced herself to envision it. Perhaps Sam would spend summers with Malik, the occasional Christmas. It would hurt, to lose her son during those times, but she could come to accept it. She recognised Sam needed a father, even if it was only a part-time one. But there would be nothing between her and Malik.

Yet even now she could feel the remembered warmth of Malik's hand on her knee, the sureness of that light touch. It made her want to lean into the caress, ask for more. She really needed to get a grip.

'I think I'll have a walk around the plane,' she said, and rose from her seat. She needed to get away from Malik. Away from her own circling, spiralling thoughts.

She strolled down the length of the plane, conscious of the stewards who deliberately didn't look at her, their faces smooth and blank. The security guards she'd seen by the door had made themselves scarce, but she was still aware of their presence on the plane. This was a whole new world she was entering, and she didn't know whether to be awed or afraid.

Eventually she ended up in the main bedroom in the back of the plane. The flight to Alazar was eighteen hours long, so she supposed they would all sleep at some point, even if she now felt too wired to so much as sit still. She pictured stretching out on that huge bed, and then before she could stop herself she pictured Malik next to her. She remembered how sinewy and powerful his body had been, muscles rippling, skin like bronzed satin under her questing hands, candlelight flickering over their naked bodies...

Stop it. You can't afford to think that way.

'Grace?' Malik appeared in the doorway of the bedroom, startling her out of her dangerous thoughts. He took a step inside and closed the door behind him, cocooning them both in the quiet luxury of the room. Gracie's gaze dropped to his powerful chest, the muscles of his arms and torso rippling under the expensive starched cotton of his shirt. A faint frown marred his sculpted features. 'Are you all right?'

Gracie tried to banish the images that were still running through her mind in a traitorous, sensual reel. 'Where's Sam?' she asked, her voice sounding strained.

'He's playing a video game in the media room.'

'Oh. Great.' She rubbed her hands over her face, fighting the sudden, stupid urge to burst into tears. She was all over the place, wanting one second, fearing the next, *feeling* too much.

'You seem disturbed,' Malik remarked, and Gracie straightened.

'No, I'm fine.' She would be. She had to get control of all these wayward feelings and wants. 'A bit overwhelmed, maybe.' Gracie tried for a laugh. 'This is the most luxurious bedroom I've ever been in. It's hard to believe it's on a plane. That bed is huge.'

'The bed is quite spacious.' Malik's voice was soft and he leaned against the door, his gaze turning hooded and sleepy. *Why* did she keep mentioning beds? 'But I remember another bed, a bed that was just as big, a room that was just as luxurious.' His gaze locked on hers and Gracie's breath bottled in her lungs.

'That was a long time ago, Malik.' Her voice sounded shaky to her own ears.

'It was, and yet right now it feels like it was yesterday. All day long I have been remembering, Grace. How you felt. How you tasted. How you responded to my touch.' He took a step towards her and Gracie froze, the blood pounding through her veins, her pulse leaping wildly in her throat. 'And,' Malik continued softly, 'I think you remember, too. Tell me you do.'

She was helpless beneath his hot gaze, everything in

her yearning. 'Yes, I do. But…' It was the feeblest resistance. She couldn't even finish the sentence.

'But?' Malik prompted. He was walking towards her with slow, sure strides. Gracie didn't move. He stopped in front of her, close enough so she could feel his heat and her body swayed helplessly towards his. 'But nothing. It is strong between us, Grace. It always has been.' He held her by the shoulders, his expression fierce and primal.

Gracie's heart started to thud hard as her body came in achingly close contact with Malik's, her breasts brushing the hard plane of his chest. 'Malik…' she whispered, her voice a plea, her head dropping back and her lips parting in blatant invitation. He was right. It was as strong as ever. Need was crashing over her in desperate waves, her body longing for his touch, her mouth demanding his kiss.

And he gave it, his mouth coming down on hers, hard and hot and yet so sweet. Gracie scrabbled at his shoulders with her hands, drawing him closer, needing the feel of his powerful body against hers. The ache in her centre intensified as she felt his arousal thrusting against her. It had been so long since she'd felt this way. Since she'd wanted someone so much, and he'd wanted her. It had been ten whole years.

Malik skimmed his hands down her body, anchoring her hips against his as he plundered her mouth. With each deliberate thrust of his body against hers, pleasure spiked through her and she moaned. Was she going to humiliate herself by falling apart at the first touch of his hands? And yet it would be so wonderful.

Through the desire-dazed fog of her brain she realised Malik had stopped moving against her. He eased away, his breath coming out in a ragged shudder. 'Not like this,' he said in a low voice. 'There is no need for us to rush.'

'But we shouldn't do this…' The sentiment sounded

paltry and token. It *was*. Because even though she knew they shouldn't, that it would be complicated and difficult, she wanted to. So much.

Malik's teeth gleamed as his mouth curved in a faint and yet proprietorial smile. 'Your argument is not convincing. But there will be time to discuss that later. For now we can enjoy each other's company in another way. A meal is being prepared in the dining room. Come and eat.'

He held out his hand, and, with her heart feeling as if it were beating its way up her throat, Gracie took his hand and let him lead her from the bedroom.

CHAPTER SEVEN

THE MOOD WAS PERFECT. Candlelight, crystal, delicious food. Sam had eaten a child's meal of chicken nuggets and chips beforehand and was happily ensconced in the media room with an array of the latest DVDs, video games and books. The jet's dining room was intimate, curtains drawn across the windows, making it feel like a private parlour in the sky. They were as alone as they could be...which was what Malik wanted.

His blood was still heated from that delicious encounter with Gracie in the bedroom. He had not anticipated seducing her so soon, and in fact he'd felt as if he'd been the one to be seduced. His desire for Gracie had overwhelmed him until he'd been acting out of base instinct and incredible need. But then so had she.

Still he needed to be careful and deliberate with his plans. He needed to convince Gracie that a convenient marriage could work between them without complicating it with emotion or love, which he suspected she would want. Somehow he would convince her of the sense and appeal of his plan. Their kiss earlier was just the beginning.

Gracie stood in the doorway of the dining room and glanced uncertainly at the crystal and silver-laid table. 'This is...nice,' she ventured, and Malik pulled out her chair.

'I'm glad you think so.'

Slowly she walked towards the chair and sat down. Malik took the liberty of placing her napkin in her lap, his fingers brushing her thighs. He felt a tremor go through her, and it gave him an almost savage satisfaction. 'You are still affected by me, Grace.'

'I think you had already figured that out.' Her breath came out in a shudder. 'Some things never change, I guess.'

'I am glad.' He sat down opposite her and poured them both wine.

Gracie eyed the glass full of ruby-red liquid askance. 'You used to call me Gracie.'

The name made him think of sweeter, more innocent times. He could not go back to being that boy again. 'Yes,' he agreed with an incline of his head, and said nothing more.

'You've changed, Malik.' The statement, given so matter-of-factly, shook him more than he cared to admit. 'Or maybe you haven't, and that boy I knew back in Rome never existed.' The tremulous note of hurt in her voice made him tense. 'We've never talked about that, you know. Why…why did you push me away? Tell me to go? I mean,' she continued in a rush, taking a sip of wine, 'I wasn't expecting hearts and roses. Well, not exactly. But I thought we shared something more special than…than it seemed in that moment.'

Malik remained silent, his mind racing as he considered how to answer her question. He hadn't expected her to be so honest, and in a reckless moment he decided to return her honesty with his own.

'We did share something unique.'

'Yeah, right.' She shook her head, clearly disbelieving, trying for bravado even though he saw an alarming vulnerability in her eyes. 'Just tell me this, at least. Was I… Was I really your first?'

A tightness formed in Malik's chest. 'Yes.' Gracie's gaze searched his face, looking for truth. 'I told you I'd lived a sheltered life, Grace. Nothing I said that night was a lie.'

'Then why were you so cold the next morning? Why did you basically boot me out of your bed? I mean, you could have given me the "it was fun, but" speech. I think I could have taken it.' Her voice wobbled slightly and she pushed a tendril of wavy golden-brown hair behind one delicate ear. 'Maybe not, though. Maybe you thought a quick cut would be better, especially with your grandfather in the room.'

'That night was like a dream to me,' Malik said slowly, choosing his words with care. 'A time out of reality. Waking up, discovering my grandfather there, that was what life was really like. And the truth was I'd acted very foolishly, being seen in public with you.'

Gracie jerked back at this. 'Ouch.'

'Not because of who you were, but who I was. Am. I could not be seen dallying with a Western woman. Such news, if it reached Alazar, had the potential to create civil unrest among my people who wanted a more traditional heir to the throne.'

'And what about now? Bringing your *Western* son back to your country? Won't that be greeted with a few raised eyebrows?'

She was quick, he had to give her that. 'Potentially, yes,' Malik said calmly. 'But the information to the public will be controlled. No one will know Sam is my son until I want them to know.'

Her eyes widened as another thought assailed her. 'Will there be publicity? For Sam? I can't stand the thought of him being hounded by the press...'

'He will not be hounded.'

'Why does anyone need to know? It's not like Sam is going to be living in Alazar.'

Malik pressed his lips together. This conversation was starting to become dangerous. 'His life has changed, Grace, as have yours and mine. We cannot pretend that is not the case.'

'I know.' She toyed with her wine glass. 'I just don't want it to change too much.'

'Don't you?' he asked quietly, and she glanced up, her eyes narrowing.

'What do you mean by that?'

Malik spread his hands, keeping his voice mild. 'You intimated before that your life was less than satisfactory. It's been hard being a single parent. Maybe there will be good changes ahead, for both of us.'

'Maybe,' Gracie allowed, and he could see she was turning that idea around in her mind. 'And maybe not.'

He decided not to push it any further for now. Gently, gently was the way forward.

'Tell me about the last ten years,' Gracie said after a moment. 'Not just the government stuff, although I know that is of course a big part.' She gave a light laugh. 'But you. What have you been doing? What are your hobbies, your interests?'

Malik blinked, entirely discomfited by such a question. 'Hobbies?' he repeated. 'I don't have any.'

'You must.'

He thought about the twenty-hour days he'd had, negotiating peace treaties with various tribes, sleeping rough, on constant alert. 'What are yours?'

'Oh. Well, I like to do needlepoint. I find it soothing.' She smiled impishly. 'You could try it.'

He smiled back, enjoying this unexpected banter. 'Perhaps I will.'

She laughed again, the rich gurgle he remembered from so long ago. 'Now I really can't picture that.'

'What else do you like to do?' Malik asked. He was genuinely curious.

'Oh, the usual. Movies, books, dinners out.' She rolled her eyes. 'I sound like I'm completing a dating profile for the Internet. I suppose I'm pretty boring.'

'Not at all.' He found her anything but.

'Gardening, when I can, although my mother is possessive about her vegetable plot.'

He thought of the extensive gardens at the royal palace, modelled on the Hanging Gardens of Babylon. 'Perhaps one day you'll have a plot of your own.'

'Yeah, maybe.' She didn't sound convinced. 'I like to spend time with Sam, really, as much as I can. Though I volunteer at the day centre for the disabled in town. And I read books to elderly people on Saturdays.'

'You sound busy.'

'I enjoy helping people. I'm never going to be a brain surgeon or something, but I like doing small things that make a difference.'

She sounded just as she had ten years ago. 'And what kind of things do you and Sam do together?'

'Anything and everything. As you might have noticed, he's a constantly moving ball of energy.' A smile curved her mouth as her face softened with love, making her even more desirable. 'He loves trivia of all kinds, especially geography. And we play board games together.' Her eyes lit up. 'There's your new hobby. Playing strategy games with your son.' Gracie paused, hesitant now, and yet also determined. 'It would be good for the two of you to spend time together, you know.'

'That is what I intend.' And yet he had not envisioned himself playing board games with his son. He had not pictured any sort of family scene; he didn't even know what one would be like. He had no reference, considering his own lonely childhood. And yet sitting here, basking in the warmth of Gracie's smile, he realised he would like to do that, very much.

Their first course came, and over a salad of couscous and cucumber Gracie asked him about Alazar. 'It sounds like a pretty harsh place. But you mentioned a capital city?'

'Yes, the royal palace is in Teruk, which is very beautiful. The Old City has some of the best preserved architecture in all of the Middle East.'

'And what about the rest of the country?'

'The interior of Alazar is mainly desert, surrounded by mountains. Inhospitable, and yet Bedouin tribes have made their home there for thousands of years.'

Gracie's smile wavered. 'And they're the source of the instability you were talking about.'

'Yes, but just before coming here I negotiated a peace. The tribes merely want to be assured that their way of life can continue.'

'And can it?' Gracie asked frankly. 'What with all the changes you are trying to make?'

'I hope it can. We cannot let all the old ways die, and there is little point in Westernising people who will live all their lives in the desert. The people of Teruk are a different matter.'

'Are they happy to modernise?'

'I believe so, yes.' Malik took a sip of wine. He was enjoying discussing these things with her, he realised. It was so different than the terse or even hostile exchanges he had with his grandfather. 'Some people, of course, welcome change more than others. There is a new school being started for young women, for example, that they are very pleased about.'

'That's good.'

'Of course, there is still a long way to go in other matters of education,' Malik continued. 'Special needs, for a start.'

Interest sparked in her eyes, as Malik had known it would. Was he manipulating her, or simply presenting a pleasing opportunity? He didn't know any more. Everything felt tangled, complicated. 'Special needs?' she repeated.

'As it happens, we have very little provision for special needs in Teruk or elsewhere in Alazar. It is something I would like to work on. Now that the country is stable, it will hopefully be possible to do so.' He paused while she considered this, and then added, 'You wanted to train as a special needs teacher, did you not?'

'Yes.' She shook her head slowly. 'It almost seems as if you remember every single thing I said that night.'

'I do.' The two words slipped out, low and so heartfelt Malik felt as if he'd exposed something he would have rather kept hidden. 'It was a magical night,' he said, an attempt to defuse the moment, but instead it only heightened it and he felt himself start to be pulled under yet again by the tide of memory that washed over him.

With the candlelight flickering between them, the room dim and hushed, he could remember just how that night had felt. How unique and wondrous it had been. And he wanted to feel it again, in its entirety. 'Walking down cobbled streets...' he said, unable to keep from saying it. 'Throwing coins in the Trevi Fountain...'

'Two coins,' Gracie recalled, her voice as low as his, her eyes blazing gold. 'For a new romance.'

'Perhaps it should have been three.' He held her gaze, letting her see the heat in his eyes, the heat he felt through his whole body. Letting her consider their future in a whole new light as desire uncoiled and snaked between them, drawing them closer, tangling them together.

Gracie broke their locked gazes first, passing a trembling hand over her face. 'Don't do this, Malik.'

'You feel it, too, Grace. *Gracie.*' He allowed himself to say her true name, the name he'd called out in his sleep more than once over the years, to his own savage frustration. 'I know you do. Back in the bedroom…'

'Of course I do.' Her breath came out in a shaky rush. 'But we can't complicate things, for Sam's sake.'

'This doesn't have to be complicated.'

She swung her gaze back to his, and now ire flashed in her lovely golden-green eyes. 'It doesn't? So what are you suggesting? Another one-night stand? Sorry, but I've been there, done that. I'm not interested.' She pushed away from the table, her lithe body taut.

'I wasn't suggesting a one-night stand. Far from it.'

'What, then?' she demanded.

Malik was silent, considering his options. He could not play his whole hand now. Gracie would reject it instinctively. There was still too much she didn't know or understand. 'All I'm asking,' he said, his voice low and steady, 'is that you keep an open mind…to all the possibilities.'

Confusion clouded her eyes. 'What possibilities? Why do I feel like you're keeping something from me? Something big?'

'The future is unknown for all of us, Grace.'

'Now we're back to *Grace*.' She shook her head, crossing her arms across her body. 'Don't lie to me, Malik. Not again.'

'I didn't lie before—'

'As good as. You should have told me you were a sultan.'

'And you should have told me you were pregnant.'

'I tried—'

'And I tried. Can we not do this? Again?'

Her body sagged. 'I'm so confused, Malik,' she whispered.

As was he. He'd enjoyed this time with Gracie, talking to her and, yes, most definitely kissing her. That had been exquisitely sweet. But such enjoyment and desire clouded what he knew in his gut had to be a business arrangement, for the sake of Alazar as well as his own.

'All will become clear eventually,' he promised. 'To both of us.' He brushed her cheek with his fingertips; her skin was impossibly soft. Letting out a shuddering breath, Gracie closed her eyes.

Gracie felt as if her emotions were in a tumble dryer; she felt a thousand things at once, and it was near impossible to separate the fear from the hope, the excitement from the uncertainty. One moment her blood had been singing with reawakened desire, and the next she was backing away in trepidation. She needed to calm down. She needed to accept this for what it was—two weeks to figure out her and Sam's next steps in life. And maybe she *could* enjoy it. Once she'd been determined to suck the marrow out of life and toss away the bones. She'd been so happy and hopeful, back in Rome. She wanted to win a little of her youthful self back.

Taking a deep breath, she smiled. 'So tell me, what are we going to do in Alazar, exactly?'

'I want to show you my country. The palaces, the capital city of Teruk and of course the mountains.'

'Sam mentioned that Alazar has the highest mountain in the Middle East.'

'Did he?' The look of pride on Malik's face made Gracie smile. 'He is a very intelligent boy.'

'He's curious. Always wanting to know more.' She took

a bite of the couscous salad and found it was delicious. As she took another mouthful, she realised how hungry she was. 'Were you like that, as a boy?'

'Once.' Malik was silent for a moment, and Gracie could tell he was considering what to tell her. How much to tell her. 'Things changed when I was twelve.'

'Why? What happened then?'

Another silence; Gracie held her breath, sensing the import of what Malik might say. Wanting to know. 'My older brother, Azim, was kidnapped then,' he explained quietly. 'And I became the heir to the throne.'

A soft gasp escaped her. 'Malik, I'm so sorry. That's terrible. What…what happened to him?'

Malik spread his hands, his powerful shoulders moving in an elegant shrug. 'No one knows. There were no ransom notes, no demands, nothing. He just disappeared, right from the palace gardens. No one saw anything.'

'I'm so sorry.' Gracie couldn't imagine that kind of loss. Her five siblings infuriated her at times, but she loved them fiercely. She couldn't imagine having one taken away so abruptly and terribly. 'Were you close to him?'

'Yes.' The single word held a world of pain. Malik looked down at his hands flat on the table. 'Yes, I was very close to him.'

'What about your parents?' She was realising afresh how little she knew about him. And she wanted to know more, to understand this intriguing and complex man.

'My mother died when I was four years old, from cancer. It was swift. My father…' He paused, and Gracie watched as he attempted to rearrange his features into the blank, hard mask she'd become familiar with. He didn't quite succeed. 'My father adored my mother. When she died, he…he lost himself. I have very few memories of him. When Azim was kidnapped…it was the final straw for him, I think. He ended up removing himself from the succession at my grandfather's request and now lives in the Caribbean. I haven't seen him since I was twelve.'

'He just abandoned you?' Gracie exclaimed, horrified by the thought.

'He was a weak man.' Malik's voice sounded hard.

So at twelve years old Malik had lost almost his whole family. Gracie was starting to understand how much he'd endured, how brutally he'd been shaped. *And how much family might mean to him.* 'So then it was just you and your grandfather,' she stated, and he nodded.

'Yes. He hadn't paid me much attention before, preferring to focus on Azim as heir. But with Azim and my father gone...' Malik shrugged. 'I needed a different education. A different life.'

'Which was?'

'The proper training and protection for an heir to the throne.'

'That's why you were so sheltered...'

'I couldn't be allowed to be kidnapped the way Azim was. I was always surrounded.'

'Which was why I was your first kiss,' Gracie whispered, and then flushed. Why had she said that? And why was she remembering the sweet slide of Malik's lips on hers, the gentle wonder of it as they'd stood by the Trevi Fountain and the whole world had seemed to fall away? And remembering more than that...the feel of his body on hers, in hers, and then just an hour ago, when he'd pressed against her so insistently and thrillingly...

'Yes,' Malik answered, his voice a low husk. The moment spun out between them, the room dim and hushed and expectant. Gracie felt her body respond, long-dormant parts of her coming alive with an insistent, pulsing ache. She took a deep breath, trying desperately to quell the tide of yearning that was now threatening to overwhelm her. She couldn't afford to feel this much now.

'Sometimes I wonder,' Malik said, his voice still low, 'what might have been.'

Gracie tried for a shaky laugh and didn't quite manage it. 'That's always dangerous.'

'I know…but don't you wonder, too, Gracie? What could have happened between us?'

'You made it clear that nothing could, Malik, when you sent me from your bed.' Yet strangely the memory didn't hurt as much as it once had.

'I had no choice. But if I had…' He left the sentence unfinished, unspoken possibilities dangling between them.

Gracie's breath hitched as she registered the intent look in Malik's eyes, felt the answering pulse of want in herself. 'We can't do this,' she whispered. 'For Sam's sake…' Unsteadily she rose from the table. 'I should go check on him.'

'I'll come with you.' Malik rose as well, tossing his napkin aside and striding towards the door. They reached it at the same time, their hands colliding on the knob, sending sparks through Gracie yet again.

How on earth could she keep resisting him, when every single simple touch set off a firework inside her?

The truth was she couldn't. With his other hand Malik turned her around so she was facing him. Gracie didn't resist as his mouth came down on hers, but instead of the wild kiss of an hour ago, this was gentle, like a promise.

His mouth moved lingeringly over hers, exploring and tasting her with thorough sensuality. She swayed on her feet as she steadied herself with one hand bunched on his shirt. Malik rested his forehead against hers.

'Let's go find Sam,' he said, and wordlessly Gracie nodded. She didn't trust herself to speak.

Sam was ensconced in the media room, playing a video game with intense concentration.

'Hey, buddy.' Gracie came over to her son, ruffling his hair, grateful for the distraction from the intensity she'd just experienced with Malik. Her lips were buzzing from that shockingly gentle kiss. 'Having fun?'

'Yeah.' Sam looked up from his game for a mere second, his eyes glinting with excitement. 'This game is one of the *best*.'

'Great.' She glanced at Malik, who was watching the two of them with that intimidatingly impassive look on his face. She didn't understand how one moment he could be so sexy and gentle, and the next look like a stranger.

'You want to play?' Sam asked Malik, holding out the controller. Malik looked taken aback.

'I don't think I've ever played this kind of game.'

Sam was flummoxed. 'You've never played a video game?'

Malik smiled faintly. 'No.'

'You haven't played that many, Sam,' Gracie felt compelled to point out. 'We don't have a play console at home.'

'And neither do I. But I might as well try.' Malik held out his hand and Sam gave him one of the controllers.

Gracie sat back and watched as Sam explained the game, all of which sounded extremely complicated, and Malik began thumbing buttons.

Who ever thought she would see this? Gracie marvelled as she watched father and son, their dark heads bent together. Her heart felt full, too full. What had Malik meant, keeping an open mind to possibilities? *What* possibilities?

Dared she think he might have meant something between them, some kind of actual relationship? The prospect sent her heart juddering. This man had just about broken her heart after a single night. Could she trust him with her entire future? She liked things as they were. Inviting Malik into her life was like walking into a whirlwind.

Sam let out a belly laugh as Malik's spaceship dived and crashed on the screen. Malik's answering smile lit up Gracie's insides. Starting to care, beginning to hope...it was all so *risky*. The pain she'd felt when Malik had turned his back on her before had been agonising. Now, if she actually tried for something real or lasting, it would be unbearable...and it would cost both her and Sam. How could she even think of such a thing?

CHAPTER EIGHT

A LEMON-YELLOW SUN shone out of a hard blue sky as they prepared for the descent into Teruk. Even after eight hours of admittedly sporadic sleep, Gracie felt wired, anticipation warring with sheer panic. Malik had generously allowed her and Sam the master bedroom, while he'd taken a pull-out sofa bed in the main cabin.

The bed had been incredibly comfortable and Sam had been out as soon as his head hit the pillow, so she couldn't blame him for her lack of sleep. No, it had been Malik who had kept her awake most of the night. Malik's sheer presence, his knowing kiss, his absolute magnetism…and the yearning desire she felt for him after all these years, as strong and powerful as it ever had been.

This morning Malik looked immaculate and refreshed, and disturbingly different in a white linen thobe and turban. The flowing clothing only emphasised his masculinity, and Gracie was conscious that she'd never before seen him in the traditional dress of his country.

'Look, Mom!' Sam was wriggling in his seat as he tried to peer out of the window. 'So many mountains.'

'Yes, indeed.' Gracie tore her gaze from Malik's powerful form to look out of the window. From the sky Alazar looked forbidding, a foreign landscape of barren mountain ranges and even more desolate stretches of desert.

The only green was on the coast, a thin crescent of arable farmland and civilisation.

'We will go directly to the palace from Teruk,' Malik told them both. He smiled at Sam. 'I cannot wait to show you.'

'Your palace?' Sam's jaw dropped. 'You have a palace?'

'I told him you worked for the government,' Gracie explained in a murmur, and Malik smiled.

'And indeed I do. My grandfather is the Sultan of Alazar, Sam, and I will be Sultan after him.'

Sam boggled. *'Wow.'*

Gracie half listened as Malik continued to tell Sam about the palace, its walls and turrets and many swimming pools. *My grandfather is the Sultan of Alazar, Sam, and I will be Sultan after him.* Just in case she'd forgotten how important he was. How surprising and scary it was for her to be here.

The plane was starting a steep descent to the runway that cut through bleak desert when Gracie refocused on Malik.

'You're all right?' he asked quietly, seeming genuinely concerned, and Gracie nodded.

'Yes.' She realised her hands were tightly gripping the armrests, and she forced herself to relax.

Moments later the plane bumped to a stop and the security guards headed for the door. Gracie rose from her seat.

'Wait.' Malik stayed her with one hand and Gracie looked at him in uneasy surprise.

'What is it?'

'I am sorry, but it is not wise for you to disembark like that.' He gestured to her clothes.

Gracie glanced down at the outfit she'd taken some time over. An Indian batik skirt in a colourful print and a modest cotton blouse that covered her shoulders and arms.

She'd been going for a casual but respectful look, but judging from Malik's frown it wasn't good enough. 'What's wrong with my clothes?' she asked.

'I'm sorry, I should have explained these arrangements earlier,' Malik said in a low voice. 'The truth is your presence in Alazar could be…disconcerting to some.'

Alarm prickled. 'Disconcerting?'

'The sudden appearance of an American woman in my life…' Malik spread his hands. 'We must take some steps to make sure the press do not have a field day with that bit of news.'

'Okay,' Gracie said cautiously. It seemed reasonable, and the less press the better as far as she was concerned, but she still felt a little wary.

'Will you wear this?' Malik asked, and held out a headscarf. Gracie looked at it dubiously for a moment.

'All right.' She took the scrap of dark fabric. 'When in Rome, I guess.' She laughed then, uncertainly, at the mention of Rome. Malik smiled faintly, and for a second it seemed as if they were in their own bubble, memories swirling between them. 'So it goes on like this?' she asked, sliding on the headscarf and drawing the tail of fabric across her neck.

'Yes…mainly.' With gentle hands Malik adjusted the scarf, his fingers whispering across her face as he moved the material. Gracie sucked in a hard breath at the brush of his hands on her skin. Somehow she was going to have to stop reacting so strongly to his touch. 'There. You look lovely.' With his hands on her shoulders he steered her to a mirror. Gracie blinked at her face, framed by the dark scarf. She looked exotic somehow, alluring even, with her hair covered and her eyes so prominent.

'You look cool, Mom,' Sam chipped in.

'I know it is not the custom for you,' Malik murmured,

his face close to hers. His hands were still on her shoulders and his breath tickled her ear. Awareness and longing rippled through her. 'Thank you for wearing it.'

Wordlessly she nodded. She didn't trust herself to say anything at that moment. She felt too many things all at once, and she had a near overwhelming instinct to lean back into Malik's solid strength.

'There is one other matter,' Malik said as he dropped his hands.

'And what is that?'

'We will need to travel in separate cars. For the sake of propriety. I will meet you at the palace. Is that acceptable?'

'I suppose,' Gracie said. Again it seemed reasonable, but with each second that they'd been in Alazar, she'd felt as if Malik was becoming more remote. His attitude was kind, and yet she sensed a coolness in him, saw it in his eyes. The man who had smiled and laughed and kissed her was gone as if he'd never been. Had it all been an act?

But maybe Malik was simply tense upon returning to his country and his duty. She certainly felt nervous about it. Straightening, she plastered a smile on her face. 'All right, are we ready to go now?'

The heat hit her like a brick wall as she stepped out of the plane. The whole world seemed to shimmer, from the flat blue sky above to the black tarmac that stretched onward to undulating sand and distant mountains. A small crowd of people was waiting by the plane, some with cameras, some with flowers and wreaths of welcome. Gracie took a deep breath and then a step forward, overwhelmed by the utter strangeness of it all. The heel of her shoe snagged on the edge of the step and for one terrifying moment she thought she was going to pitch forward and fall flat on her face. Welcome to Alazar.

Malik reached out one hand and grabbed her elbow in

an iron grip, steadying her as she made her way down the steep steps. She could hear the murmur of voices from the crowd like the buzz of bees. This was already so much more than she'd expected.

'Almost there,' Malik said in a low voice. Sam was looking around with wide eyes. In front of her she could see a blacked-out sedan, the door thankfully open.

Cameras clicked and people jabbered questions in Arabic. Gracie stared straight ahead, wanting only the safety and privacy of the car.

And then thankfully she was sliding inside next to Sam. Malik leaned in, his face close to hers. 'I'll see you at the palace.'

What had seemed reasonable before now felt frightening. She wanted him with her, taking her through all this strangeness.

'Not long, I promise,' Malik said, and with that he was gone.

The car sped away, desert stretching on either side, the dark, craggy mountains thrusting up towards a brilliant blue sky. It was beautiful, yet stark. Gracie took a deep breath and turned to Sam.

'So,' she said. 'This is Alazar.'

'Yeah, isn't it cool?' Sam scooted closer to the window. 'Which is Mount Jebar, do you think?'

'Mount what?'

'The highest mountain in Alazar.'

'I don't know. Maybe Malik will tell us.' Gracie glanced at the driver, his face as impassive as Malik's ever was, his eyes hidden by dark sunglasses. She clasped her hands together and remembered the feel of Malik's hand on hers. The warmth of his body next to hers. It was going to be okay.

Ten minutes later the sedan pulled up to a magnificent

palace of golden stone that seemed to stretch for miles in every direction. Through the tinted windows Gracie could make out domes and spires and a huge Moorish arched entrance, surrounded by landscaped gardens and fountains.

'Wow,' she breathed, because the whole thing was amazing. Her nerves relented a little as she took in the fairy-tale scene. She felt as if she should pinch herself.

The car pulled around to a side door and the driver got out and then opened the passenger door, gesturing with one hand for her to exit.

'His Highness wishes for you to remain comfortable while you wait for him,' he said in flawless English. 'Please let me know if there is anything you desire. Anything at all.'

'Thank you,' Gracie murmured. All she wanted was Malik. She followed the driver to a set of double doors of intricately latticed wood. He bowed and indicated she should proceed.

A beautiful mosaic-tiled corridor led to an open courtyard with a fountain and several stone benches carved into the ancient walls. A table and chairs had been set up under a white linen awning, with a pitcher of fruit juice and a bowl of sticky dates and figs. The only sound was the soothing tinkle and splash of the water in the fountain.

'This is so cool,' Sam said, and reached for a fig.

'Sam…' It was a warning, although she wasn't sure why. What were the manners for a time and place such as this?

'Please,' the man said. 'Help yourself. A servant will be with you shortly to see to your every need. In the meantime, if there is anything else you require…'

'No,' Gracie said after a second's pause. Her head was still spinning. 'No, thank you.'

The man bowed again and left them alone, the doors clicking shut behind him.

'Are we actually staying here?' Sam exclaimed. 'This is amazing.'

'I…I guess so.' Four doors led off the courtyard, each through intricate Moorish arches. Gracie felt her spirits lift as her curiosity was piqued. 'Maybe we should explore.'

'Definitely,' Sam agreed, and together they went through one of the arches. It led to an elegant salon with louvered shutters open to the fresh, orange-blossom-scented air. Gracie took in the low divans scattered with silken pillows, the bouquets of fresh flowers and bowls of fruit. It was a lovely, peaceful place, and she could picture herself curled up on one of the sofas with a book. *With Malik.*

Sam tugged on her hand and they went through the other rooms—a bedroom with a huge king-sized bed and a gorgeous en-suite bathroom. The sunken marble tub was the size of a small swimming pool.

Through the next door there *was* a swimming pool, with a sauna and whirlpool and a small private gym. The final door led to another bedroom, just as sumptuous as the other.

'Is this all for us?' Sam asked in a near whisper.

'It seems like it.'

Gracie heard the sound of a door opening, and she turned to see a smiling young woman coming down the corridor that must have led to the rest of the palace. Gracie smiled back, trying to quell the disappointment that it wasn't Malik.

'Good afternoon. It is my pleasure to serve you,' the woman said. 'My name is Leila.' She dipped a small curtsey and then hurried about, fetching them glasses of juice, insisting they needed to sit down and relax.

'Would madam like some spa treatments?' she suggested. 'A massage or facial to relax?'

'Oh, wow.' Gracie hadn't had a spa treatment—ever. 'Thank you…um…maybe later.'

'Something else to drink, or to eat? Whatever you would like…'

'Can I have ice cream?' Sam asked impulsively.

'Sam…' Gracie interjected.

'Of course,' the woman said easily. 'What flavour?'

'Um… Rocky Road?'

'Of course.'

Gracie felt as if they'd entered some twilight zone where your every wish was granted. Had she inadvertently sold her soul?

Maybe.

'Excuse me, but could you tell me when Ma—um… the…that is, His Highness Malik al Bahjat is going to be back?'

The woman's face clouded briefly. 'I am afraid I do not know. He is in a meeting with his fiancée's father.'

His *what*? Gracie blinked. 'His fiancée?' she repeated slowly.

'Her father, yes. The wedding is in a few months.' The woman's smile was restored. 'We have not had a royal wedding in many years.'

'How exciting,' Gracie managed. She couldn't untangle the feelings that were snaking through her, but none of them felt good. From somewhere, she managed a stiff smile. 'Please offer His Highness my congratulations.'

Tension banded Malik's temples as he strode into one of the palace's formal salons, where Arif Behwar waited. He wanted to be with Gracie, and the last thing he'd needed was hearing that not only was Asad ill and bedridden, but his fiancée's father had paid an unexpected visit and was waiting for him.

'Arif.' Malik inclined his head in a greeting. 'This is a surprise.'

'As was news of your trip to America, and the fact that you returned with a woman and child,' Arif returned tersely. 'Considering you are to marry my daughter in a few months, I am naturally concerned.'

So they hadn't been able to fly under the radar after all. Malik carefully closed the door behind him. 'What did you hear?'

'Just that. You flew very suddenly to the States, and just as suddenly returned. Who is she, Your Highness?' The honorific was bitten off and flung at him.

Malik's mouth compressed. He had wanted to postpone the news of who Gracie and Sam were until things were more secure. Until he was married to Gracie and Sam was legitimised.

'I am afraid,' he said carefully, 'my situation has changed.'

Arif's scowl deepened. 'In what way?'

'I can no longer marry your daughter.'

'We had an agreement—'

'I have recently discovered I am infertile.' The news, so starkly given, silenced the older man. It made Malik's stomach clench unpleasantly, as well. Infertile. Would he ever get used to that? How would Gracie react? The one thing he would never give her was children…or his love. And knowing her, she might want both. His resolve hardened into a metal ball in his gut. He would simply have to convince Gracie of all the things he could give her…and that they would be enough.

'Infertile,' Arif repeated after a long, tense moment. 'What will this do to our country?'

He was, Malik noted, more concerned for Alazar than for his daughter Johara. 'Nothing, I hope. My infertility is a recent occurrence, due to a fever I sustained in the desert.' He paused, debating how much to reveal even as he acknowledged that one of his top government officials needed to know the truth. 'The boy I arrived with today is my son.'

Arif's eyebrows rose. 'Your son? Your bastard, you mean.'

Cold fury rippled through him. 'Do not insult my heir.'

Arif ignored him. 'And the woman? That is his mother?'

'That,' Malik informed him in a tone of silky menace, 'is soon to be the Sultana.'

Arif stepped back, shocked. 'You intend to marry her?'

'Of course.'

Arif's face twisted. 'The Bedouin will rebel. They will not want a Western sultana, and what of a Western sultan one day—'

'They will accept. They will have to accept.' Malik spoke flatly, brooking no disagreement. This was going to happen. He would make sure of it.

'You do not know what you are doing, Your Highness,' Arif said.

'I am doing what I must,' Malik answered, 'and that is all you need to know.' With a terse nod he dismissed the man.

A few minutes later, thankfully free of his former fiancée's father, Malik went in search of Gracie and Sam. He'd given instructions for them to be taken to the more private and secure quarters in the east wing, and given whatever they desired. He hoped they'd been able to amuse themselves in his absence, and that Gracie hadn't started to worry as he knew she was prone to do, considering the circumstances.

He heard splashing as he entered the enclosed harem where his mother had once resided. It had been empty for decades, and it brought a faint smile to his face to hear the sounds of fun and laughter, as well as a pang for the distant days he barely remembered, when his mother had been alive. When he'd felt part of a family.

Sam was swimming in the pool, with Gracie sitting on the side, her bare feet dangling in the water, her long golden-brown hair falling in tumbled waves about her shoulders. She'd taken off the headscarf and Malik couldn't say he missed it. He loved her hair.

She glanced up as Malik entered, the smile sliding off her face.

'Hello.' She sounded cool, reserved. Malik hesitated, discomfited by the sudden change in her expression.

'You have been comfortable?'

'Fine, thank you.'

Why so cold? he wondered. What had happened? 'And your quarters are pleasing?'

'How could they not be?'

Malik came closer, trying to untangle what was going on as well as to suppress the spike of irritation he felt at her inexplicable distance. 'Then everything is well?' he asked after a moment.

'Fine,' Gracie answered, her voice brittle. 'Except...' She took a shuddering breath, her golden-green gaze now full of hurt and accusation. 'I just wondered when you were going to tell me about your fiancée.'

CHAPTER NINE

As soon as Gracie asked the question, she wished she hadn't. It made her sound needy, when she *wasn't*. She was just…confused. Yesterday Malik had kissed her and then asked her to be open to all the possibilities. Maybe she'd misread the situation entirely, which she'd done before. The thought made her feel both humiliated and hurt.

Malik's mouth compressed and his gaze flicked to Sam splashing in the water. 'This is not the time for that particular discussion.'

'When, then?' Gracie demanded. 'I mean…' she lowered her voice to an accusatory hiss '…it doesn't matter to me. But you have no business kissing me the way you did when you're getting married in a couple of *months*!'

Malik's nostrils flared. 'I am not getting married in a couple of months.'

'What… You're not?' Now she felt completely wrong-footed. 'But you *are* engaged.'

'I *was*.'

'Hey, are you going to swim with us?' Sam called.

'I would like that very much,' Malik answered. He gave Gracie a quelling look. 'We will have this discussion at another, more appropriate time.'

Feeling both chastised and frustrated, Gracie nodded and went to find her swimsuit. A few minutes later all three of them were in the pool, swimming and splashing around. The sight of Malik in a pair of navy-blue swim trunks was enough to steal Gracie's breath; she'd forgotten how magnificent his body was, all bronzed, lean, tapered muscle.

As he roughhoused with Sam, she noticed marks she didn't think had been there when she'd last seen him shirtless—a scar on the side of his torso and another by his knee. They looked as if they had been serious injuries, and she wondered what on earth could have caused them.

What kind of life had Malik been living these last ten years or, really, his whole life? He'd shared intriguing details, hints at a lonely childhood and an adulthood devoted to duty that gave Gracie a sorrowful twist even as she wondered if Sam—if she and Sam—could bring a new joy into Malik's life.

Not if he's engaged.

The reality, Gracie knew, was she'd been half imagining some ridiculous happily-ever-after among Malik's *possibilities*. She hadn't articulated it to herself until she'd heard Malik was engaged and realised what a fantasyland she'd been subconsciously living in.

Of course Malik was going to marry someone else. Some modest, traditional woman who'd most likely been brought up to be a sultan's bride since she was a baby. Of course he would have other children with that oh-so suitable wife. Of course Sam would only ever be on the periphery of his life, and she even more so. The realisation should not have brought the tearing sense of grief and loss that she so shamingly felt. Malik had been back in her life for only a few days.

But he never left your heart.

'So what's it like to be Sultan?' Sam asked when they were sprawled on loungers after swimming. Another staff member had brought fresh pomegranate juice and a plate of sticky, delicious pastries made with honey and studded with nuts.

'Hmm, that is an interesting and difficult question.' Malik leaned back in his lounger and Gracie tried not to stare at the perfect musculature of his chest beaded with sparkling droplets of water. She remembered how hot and hard and satiny his skin had felt against her palm. 'It's busy, I suppose, and sometimes it feels pressured. But it is also very rewarding to serve my people, and to help to improve their living conditions.'

Sam nodded seriously. 'And you get to live in this palace.'

Malik's eyes glinted with humour as he nodded back. 'Yes, there is that.'

'Do you mind?' Sam asked. 'The pressure? Everyone looking up to you and stuff?'

'Sometimes. But I have found ways to deal with it.'

'How?'

Gracie leaned forward, curious to hear Malik's answer.

'Well,' Malik answered slowly, 'if I'm feeling worried about something, I try to find a way to relax. I walk or swim or sometimes I read.'

'And here I thought you didn't have any hobbies,' Gracie teased. Malik inclined his head in acknowledgement.

'I believe you had suggested needlepoint.'

'Read? I like to read,' Sam said. 'What kinds of things do you read?'

Gracie was intrigued to see a faint blush appear on Malik's cheeks. 'To relax, light mysteries.' He gave Gracie a wry and almost embarrassed look. 'I find whodunits are a pleasant escape from reality.'

A gurgle of surprised laughter escaped her. 'Nothing beats a good Agatha Christie.'

'Exactly.'

She eyed him appraisingly for a few seconds. 'I didn't know that about you.'

'I suspect there are many things you don't know about me,' Malik said quietly.

A few minutes later Sam went to investigate the suite's selection of DVDs and Gracie and Malik were left alone.

Nerves fluttered like trapped birds in her chest and she took a sip of juice to steel herself to ask the question that she needed to, even if she'd rather chat about books or banter about hobbies. 'So, are you or are you not engaged?'

'I am not.' Malik folded his arms across his impressive chest, biceps rippling. 'As I said before.'

'But the woman who served us said the royal wedding was in a couple of months. I don't think she got the memo.'

'I *was* engaged,' Malik clarified, 'and I broke the engagement today.'

Gracie was silent for a moment, absorbing this fact. 'Why did you break it?' she finally asked.

'Because of you. And Sam.' Malik met her gaze directly, his expression serious, composed and very determined. Gracie shrank inwardly at the hardness she saw in his eyes, even though she didn't know why it was there.

'But why would you…?'

'Because Sam is my heir.' Malik paused, his gaze fierce and dark and unrelenting. 'He will be Sultan of Alazar after me.'

For one ludicrous second Gracie pictured her impish son in robes and a crown, a jewelled sceptre in his hand, like some kind of Halloween costume. 'Whoa. *Whoa.*' She held up one hand, fighting the urge to give in to a sudden fit of hysterical laughter. 'What are you talking about? Sam can't be your *heir.*'

An eyebrow arched. 'Why not?'

'Because…' She shook her head, her mind spinning.

She'd imagined all sorts of scenarios, but she hadn't expected *this*. 'You're only what? Thirty-two?' A terse nod was all the confirmation she got. 'You could still marry and have children,' she said, even though she didn't enjoy pointing out that particular fact. 'You don't need Sam to be your heir.'

Malik didn't speak for a moment. His shuttered gaze rested on the desert and mountain vista visible through the arched windows. He'd placed his hands flat on his thighs, so Gracie could see his long, tapered fingers, and her body remembered how those hands had felt, finding her secret places. How loving and thorough they'd been. She banished the memory, refocusing on his face. *Not helpful now, Gracie.*

'Two months ago I was in the desert,' Malik said, which seemed apropos of nothing. Gracie stared at him, waiting for the blanks to be filled in. 'I became ill and ran a high fever. Being far from any medical facility, I had the fever for several days.' He stopped, looking down at his hands, his expression still closed. Gracie was just about to ask what any of this had to do with her and Sam when Malik raised his gaze and stared at her bleakly. 'Four days ago I learned that the fever had made me infertile. Sam is and will always be my only child.'

The words hit her like hammer blows. She blinked, trying to take it all in. 'I'm sorry,' she said at last, meaning it utterly, because that had to have been devastating to discover. Malik inclined his head briefly.

'Thank you.'

'That news must have been…' she shook her head slowly '…hard.'

'Yes.'

'And your fiancée…?' Gracie ventured. 'Did she…?'

'That is why I terminated the agreement. I doubted she

would want to continue, considering my state. A woman's joy and pride is her children, especially in a country like mine. But in any case Johara and I barely knew each other. We have only met twice.'

That shouldn't have made her feel better, but it did. And yet... Sam was his only child. His *heir*. The dazed feeling evaporated like mist. 'No,' she blurted.

Malik's dark eyes narrowed. 'No?' he repeated softly.

'No. Sam is— He can't be some *sultan*. The idea is ridiculous. He's a fifth-grader who's only left Illinois twice. He can't... He isn't prepared. I don't want him to be prepared. I don't want to put that pressure on him...the pressure you were just talking about.'

'I will prepare him.'

'It's impossible,' Gracie insisted even though she felt as if she were already sliding down a slippery and inexorable slope. Eventually she'd land at the bottom with an almighty thud.

Malik was silent for a long, tense moment, his hard stare seeming to take her full measure. 'Improbable, yes,' he said at last. 'Unbelievable, even.' His gaze pinned her in place. 'But not impossible.' There was steel in his voice, in his eyes, and Gracie came up against it hard.

'And if I refuse?' she asked in a low voice. 'If I say no to all of this and take Sam back to America...'

Malik narrowed his gaze to silver slits. 'Is that a threat?'

'It feels like you're the one threatening me.' How had they got to this place? Moments ago she'd been berating herself for embroidering some fantasy that involved her, Malik and Sam forming some version of happy families. Now they'd reached this terrible precipice, and Gracie had no idea how far the drop was, or how hard the landing. It was as if a kaleidoscope had turned, shaking everything up and creating an entirely new and unwelcome picture. *Sultan.* She wasn't ready for that, not for Sam, and not for her.

'There is no threat,' Malik stated. 'But there is the reality that Sam is my heir. Sam's legacy is the sultanate of Alazar. You cannot deny him his heritage. Indeed, I do not think you would even wish to.'

Gracie swallowed hard. 'You can't just spring this on me, Malik, and expect me to accept it instantly, no question...'

'Gracie.' Malik's voice turned gentle, tugging at her. 'Surely this did not come as a complete surprise. You must have realised something of this.'

'No.' She shook her head, the movement almost violent. 'No, I never thought...I imagined that you'd have Sam to visit, or maybe come to Illinois...' She trailed off, because even to her those scenarios now sounded ludicrous. Malik didn't belong in Illinois. She couldn't expect him to simply slot into her life...and yet he was asking her to slot into his. 'I don't know what I expected, but not *this*. I mean, will the people of Alazar even accept Sam? They sound so traditional and he's American. You'll be springing this on them as much as on me, and they might not like it. They might rebel like they did before.'

'True. He will have to be introduced to my people very carefully.'

'And what about his life back in Illinois...?'

'I have no intention of cutting him off from his family,' Malik interjected swiftly. 'There can always be visits.'

Visits. Gracie stared at him, shocked at just how much Sam's life—and hers—had changed. Utterly. Irrevocably. And resistance felt futile. Malik leaned over and rested one hand on her bare knee.

'I realise this is a surprise. But you must see it is the right way, the only way.'

'I must?' Because she didn't know what else to do, she railed against his autocratic tone. 'I don't think I *must* do anything. I came for a two-week visit.' Gracie heard her voice becoming high. 'And at the end of two weeks, I'm taking Sam back to America. That's what we agreed on.'

Malik withdrew his hand. The gentleness she'd seen so briefly in his eyes had vanished. When he spoke, his voice was soft and yet as lethal as a blade. 'Do not threaten me, Grace.'

'I'm stating facts—'

'Then I shall state one, as well. Did you even look at that document you signed ten years ago?'

Gracie stared at him, her jaw slack, her mind scrambling. She pictured the paper Asad had shoved at her, her quick, desperate scrawl. 'Yes,' she managed. 'It said that I couldn't contact you or anyone in Alazar ever again.'

'It also said,' Malik informed her, 'that you acknowledged me as the child's father, and gave me permission to take him to Alazar should I require his presence.'

'What?' Gracie gaped at him. 'But I didn't read that—'

'Perhaps you should have been more careful,' Malik replied, 'before you took your payoff.'

She recoiled, stung by his sneering words as much as this new, unwelcome revelation. Malik took a deep breath. 'I don't want to fight you,' he said.

'But you will if you have to?' Gracie finished. 'I get it now. All the nice stuff, all the smiles and kindness and the...the *kissing*...it was just you manipulating me to get what you want.' Malik didn't reply and Gracie clambered off the lounger, feeling sick. 'At least now I know the truth.'

Malik's face was closed as he said, 'It isn't like that, Grace.'

'How is it, then?' she demanded.

'I admit, the circumstances are less than ideal and there

is much for each of us to adjust to. But consider Sam for a moment. Consider the legacy he has been given, the *privilege*.'

'You never seemed to think it was a privilege,' Gracie retorted. 'I remember back in Rome you said you chafed at the restraints of your duty. You didn't even seem like you wanted to be Sultan.'

As soon as she said it, Gracie knew she'd gone too far. Malik's mouth compressed, his features pinched. 'I will always do my duty,' he said in a low voice, and she realised she'd actually hurt him with those words. 'As Sam should do his. Do you know how important securing the sultanate is? My country has been unstable for years. Ensuring my dynasty is crucial, not just to Alazar, but to the whole region, and even the world. You might think I am being melodramatic, but I assure you I am not.'

Gracie stared at him, his eyes blazing icy fire, colour slashing his high cheekbones. 'But he's just a little boy,' she whispered.

'And he will not be Sultan for a long time, God willing. But his place belongs here, with me.'

'And what about me?' Gracie asked, her voice a thread of sound. She had a sudden, horrible vision of Sam living in Alazar, while she came in for flying visits. *She* was the one who would have the visits, instead of her son. 'Where is my place, Malik?' Her voice throbbed with both fear and fury.

Malik's gaze did not waver as he answered. 'Your place is here, as well,' he said. 'With me.'

Malik watched as Gracie processed this information. Her face was flushed, her eyes flashing gold, her damp hair tumbling about her shoulders in unruly ringlets. She looked magnificent.

'What do you mean?' she asked unsteadily. 'Are you going to stash me in some room in the palace? The *harem*?'

'Actually,' Malik said mildly, 'this *is* the harem.'

'What...?'

'Did you know harem actually means forbidden place...?'

'Oh, great!'

'Because it is sacred. It is for the women's privacy and modesty, not to keep them imprisoned.'

She folded her arms, defensive, fearful and yet still coming out swinging. 'That's just a fringe benefit, then?'

'You are not imprisoned, Gracie,' Malik said quietly, although he knew that was not quite the truth. He could not let her leave Alazar. Not yet, anyway. If she chose to leave after they were married, she would be leaving Sam, and he knew she would never do that. She *was* a prisoner, in that sense, and he felt an uncomfortable twisting of guilt in his middle.

Of course, at some point it had had to come to this. Peel away the flattery and the kisses, delightful as they were, and the reality was they had to marry no matter what. He could dress it up with flattery and flirting and seduction, but that hard reality would never change. He couldn't care what she thought. Her feelings didn't matter.

'Listen,' he said, and Gracie's eyes narrowed in suspicion. 'Give us all a chance to adjust. Let me show you my country, my people, and keep an open mind. There is so much good you could do here, Grace.'

'Good...?'

'Let's the three of us go on a tour of Teruk tomorrow,' Malik suggested. 'I will show you the city's sights, its heritage. And we can spend some time getting to know one another.' The more he spoke, the more he liked the idea. He needed Gracie to relax and open up...and he knew he'd enjoy being with her. Already he could see her starting to soften and he reached for her hand. She didn't resist although he could tell she'd thought about it and so he tugged her towards him. 'You are tired and jet-lagged and so much has been sprung on you. Relax tonight with Sam, and tomorrow let's spend the day together. The future will take care of itself.'

'You make it sound so easy,' Gracie grumbled, but with each tug on her hand she was coming towards him, until she was standing before him, her hips bumping his.

'Maybe this *can* be easy,' Malik murmured. He tucked a few strands of hair behind her ears, unable to resist letting his fingers trail along her neck. He felt a tremor go through her and he dropped his fingers lower, to her breastbone, his fingertips skimming the tops of her breasts. Another tremor went through her.

'There is so much we could enjoy,' Malik murmured. 'So much we could do together...' He pressed his mouth to the curve of her neck and felt Gracie sag against him.

'Don't...' she whispered, her eyes fluttering closed. 'I know what you're doing. You're trying to weaken my resistance...'

'Is it working?' he murmured as he moved his mouth lower, over the damp swimming costume, his tongue teasing the aching peak of her breast. Gracie groaned aloud.

'This isn't fair,' she muttered, and Malik let out a ragged laugh.

'Fair? Do you know what you do to me, Gracie? You haven't even touched me and I'm on fire.' He brought her hand to his chest so she could feel the thud of his heart. Without even trying, *she* was able to seduce *him*. A dangerous notion he would have to keep in check.

Gracie's eyes widened and she pressed her hand harder against his chest. 'I'm scared, Malik.'

Her admission, so honestly given, undid him in a whole new and disturbing way. He covered her hand with his own. 'Why be scared?' he asked softly. 'This could be an adventure, Gracie, just as you always wanted. The greatest adventure of all…for both of us.' As he said the words, he saw her face soften, the tentative hope light her eyes. He knew he was saying what she wanted to hear, but, unsettlingly, he believed it.

Half an hour later Malik left Gracie and Sam resting in the harem while he went in search of Asad. Gracie had made no promises, but he thought he'd defused the worst of her resistance. She had agreed to sightsee in Teruk with him and Sam tomorrow, and Malik hoped she would begin to realise the possibilities she could have here.

And as for him…? The idea of stashing Gracie in some distant palace as Asad had once suggested was repellent to him now. He wanted her with him, in his bed—and in his life, Sultana to his Sultan. As for these feelings she awoke in him…this protectiveness and affection and desire… Was this what his father had felt for his mother? Was this a weakness, a canker that would work its way through his heart and soul and leave him empty and powerless?

No. He would not let that happen. A convenient marriage, he determined, could still be an enjoyable one. There was nothing to keep him and Gracie from enjoying all of its benefits…without risking their hearts.

Asad was resting in his bedroom, and Malik paused on the threshold of the spartan chamber—his grandfather had always eschewed personal luxuries or even comforts as a sign of weakness—and observed the elderly man lying propped up in bed.

Asad lifted one claw-like hand as he gestured to himself. 'As you can see, I am incapacitated today.'

Malik sketched a bow of obeisance. 'I am sorry to hear it.'

Asad let out a rasping laugh. 'Are you? Or are you pleased that the crown will soon be on your head, the sceptre in your hand?'

Malik kept his expression neutral as he replied, 'You are not as ill as that, I hope.'

'I have cancer,' Asad said flatly. He looked away, his chin jutting out, his lips pursed. 'I've known for several months. There's nothing the doctors can do. I'm too old for treatment.'

Shock kept Malik from replying for several seconds. He'd known his grandfather was elderly and becoming more frail, but he had not guessed it was as serious as this. 'I am sorry,' he said at last. 'Truly.' He realised he meant it—Asad was the only family he had, the only parental figure he'd really known. Their relationship had been marked by hostility and harshness, but it had still been a relationship. It had mattered. Asad had stayed when his father had left, had *chosen* to leave him, to retreat from life because of a broken heart.

Asad lifted a bony shoulder in a shrug. 'We all must serve our time and accept our due. I am not afraid of death.' He turned back to pierce Malik with a dark and forbidding glare. 'But I wish to have the succession firmly in place before I leave this earth.'

'Of course.'

'The boy is here?'

'Yes.'

'And the mother?'

'Yes.' Malik said nothing more; he did not want to talk about Gracie with Asad.

'I wish to meet him.'

'Of course, in time. He does not yet know I am his father.'

'Why not?' Asad demanded before gesturing to his wasted body. 'As you can see, there is little time to lose.'

'This must be handled carefully for the sake of the crown.'

'You are too soft,' Asad scoffed. 'You are already soft on the boy, I can tell. Just like your father.'

Except his father had not been soft with him, not really. After those few foggy memories of childhood, his father had maintained his distance—and then left completely. As for *the boy*... Yes, perhaps he was soft on Sam. Because he knew what being hard felt like and it had done nothing but embitter him. Still he resisted the implication, the criticism. He'd heard it far too often, been mocked and berated for being *soft*. He would not be soft, not when it mattered. Not with Gracie.

CHAPTER TEN

IT WAS ANOTHER BRIGHT, hot day when Gracie, Sam and Malik headed out to explore the city of Teruk. Malik had smiled in approval at Gracie's modest sundress and headscarf, and Sam had rolled his eyes.

'You're really taking this "when in Rome" thing seriously, Mom,' he said.

'That's right,' Gracie answered lightly. 'Don't you forget it.'

After spending several hours staring up at the ornate ceiling last night, her mind going in useless circles, she'd decided to let the day speak for itself. There was simply too much to process from what Malik had said to what he hadn't said, and without knowing everything all she could do was worry. What place would she have in Malik's life? What would Sam's life look like? Would he go to school? Could he still be a regular little boy? And if she lived in Alazar, what on earth would she *do*?

By sheer determination she had pushed the questions aside and eventually dropped off to sleep, only to wake up this morning and have them crowd in again. It took another big effort to stop from worrying them over like a dog with a well-chewed bone, but now, after a pleasant breakfast of pastries and coffee with both Sam and Malik in the palace's splendid gardens, she was looking forward to exploring the city—and spending time with Malik.

Malik was in good spirits, dressed in a more casual thobe, his skin bronzed and gleaming against the cream linen, chatting to Sam about the history of Teruk as they were driven into the city. Sam was soaking it all up like a sponge, his curiosity as insatiable as ever.

Gracie sat back and enjoyed the view of the ancient cobbled streets and wide, sweeping squares, many with fountains in their centres, as she half listened to Malik talk about a resounding victory against the Ottoman Empire in the thirteen-hundreds, when the soldiers of Alazar camped in the mountains and ate their horses when they'd run out of food.

'We are a strong and independent people,' he said, with a hand on Sam's shoulder. 'We always have been.'

'And stubborn?' Gracie teased, and Malik gave her an answering smile.

'That, too.'

The palace was in Teruk's old city, although Gracie glimpsed a few glittering skyscrapers in the distance. Malik followed her gaze. 'Mainly banking,' he said. 'I am trying to promote industry and trade with the West.'

'And is it working?'

'Yes. Alazar has been very traditional, but any country must adapt to keep up with the times.'

'So where are we going exactly?' Gracie asked. 'What are you showing us?'

'A little slice of life in Alazar. The city's university, one of the oldest in the Middle East, and then the park and a school and the marketplace. I hope you will enjoy it.'

'I'm sure I will.' Already Gracie found she was enjoying being out and about; all the new and different sights were both interesting and invigorating, the sense of adventure she had, out of necessity, had to suppress stirring to life once more, enough to keep her earlier concerns at bay.

A few minutes later the car stopped in front of a large, ancient building with three sets of Moorish arches and lavish mosaic-tiled floors.

'This bit is a museum now,' Malik explained. 'But the university is still active, with a thousand students.'

'Men?' Gracie guessed, and Malik smiled in rueful acknowledgement.

'Mostly men, but we have had a few women gain admission in the last few years. It is something I am pushing to see much more of.'

'There are schools for girls?' Gracie asked, and Malik's smile deepened.

'I thought you might ask me about that.'

They toured the university, poring over ancient manuscripts and artefacts that were both beautiful and exotic. A lecturer at the university, who spoke flawless English and gave both Gracie and Sam a warm welcome, ushered them to a courtyard filled with orange trees and the gentle tinkling of water splashing in an ornate fountain. They were served mint tea and Gracie asked questions about the education system in Alazar, gratified to hear about the reforms that Malik was having put in place.

'You've done a lot for this country,' she said quietly as they got back in the car.

'There is always more to do. And unfortunately my position has been more about dealing with military concerns than matters of education or business.'

'Is that what you're more interested in? Education and business?'

Malik shrugged. 'It is my duty to be interested in all of it.'

They left the university to explore Teruk's park on the

outskirts of the city, a huge green space with surprisingly modern facilities for sport and leisure.

Gracie watched as Malik and Sam played an Arabic version of boules, rolling stone balls down a manicured lawn with grass like green velvet. With their dark heads bent together, it was impossible not to see they were father and son. She wondered if the security guards watching discreetly from the edges of the park noticed. When would Malik tell Sam about his future? When would he tell her about hers? Because more and more she was realising her life was truly in Malik's hands…she could and would try to exert control, but it felt like fighting against the tide.

Seeing him smiling now, tousling Sam's hair in a gesture of unusually easy affection, Gracie wondered if something could work between them all. If they could be a family of sorts. The possibility felt both outrageous and overwhelming. *What was she really thinking? Hoping for?* She was afraid to articulate it even to herself.

When Malik had mentioned possibilities, love definitely hadn't seemed like one of them. Even when he was smiling or laughing—or kissing her—he seemed closed off, as if he was hiding part of himself from her. And did she even want love? Love was so risky. Her one experience of anything close to it had just about devastated her. Could she really be contemplating trying again—and with the same man who had hurt her so badly before? It sounded like insanity.

Malik glanced back to smile at her, and Gracie's thoughts scattered. She couldn't think of anything sensible when he looked at her like that.

After the park they stopped at a modest building on a side street near the Old City. A smiling woman in Western dress and a headscarf came out to greet them, making obeisance to Malik before she turned to Gracie with a smile.

'His Highness mentioned that you had a particular interest in the education of Alazar's girls and women. I am so glad to hear it.'

'He…did?' Gracie threw Malik a questioning glance, but he merely smiled blandly. Uncertainly she followed the woman into the building. It took only a moment for her to realise it was a girls' school, and she spent a happy hour watching lessons, talking to teachers in a mixture of pantomime and broken English, learning about the strides they were making in education.

'That was really interesting,' she said when they were back in the car and Sam was busy looking out of the window at a market square full of people, from snake charmers to a dentist with a basket of pulled teeth by his feet. 'Thank you for arranging it.'

'I'm glad you enjoyed it,' Malik returned. 'You certainly looked like you did,' he added, a smile in his voice. 'I have not seen your eyes sparkle so much since Rome.'

Gracie laughed, discomfited and yet flattered, too. 'Thank you, I think.'

Malik leaned towards her. 'There is a place for you in Alazar, Gracie.'

Her heart felt as if it were lurching up into her throat. 'Yes, but what kind of place?' She looked away, not sure she was ready to hear the answer. 'We can't talk about this now.'

'No,' Malik agreed. 'But soon. Very soon.'

His implacable tone gave Gracie a shiver of apprehension. Were his words a promise or a threat? She wasn't ready to have that conversation, not when she didn't know how she felt herself.

As the day progressed, Gracie turned what Malik had said over in her mind. *Was* there a place for her here? Could she get involved, maybe even make a difference in a way she hadn't been able to in Addison Heights, championing the schools for girls, perhaps pioneering special needs education? The thought intrigued and excited her in a way little had in the last ten years. She had a place in Addison Heights, but it sometimes felt small and limited, with few prospects beyond working her part-time job and being the Jones kid who had messed up. Could things be different in Alazar? Could she recapture the young girl she'd once been, full of hope and crazy dreams?

'Do you think your people will accept an American?' Gracie asked when they were seated on the roof terrace of a café overlooking the square, glasses of refreshing mint tea placed in front of them. Sam was practically hanging off the side, a security guard hovering nearby, trying to glimpse the sights in the market square below.

'I think in time,' Malik answered. 'Admittedly some of my people will have to be dragged into the modern age kicking and screaming, but I still intend for it to happen.'

'And what of your grandfather?' Gracie asked, lowering her voice even though Sam wasn't listening. 'I see what you're doing, Malik. You're showing me that I could have some sort of life in Alazar. While Sam is Sultan-in-Training, I could involve myself in charitable works, have a purpose, maybe more of one than I do in Illinois.' She sighed, her gaze on the minarets in the distance. 'And honestly, it's almost tempting. Coming here has made me realise how stuck I'd become back home.'

'It is not a waste, to be a good mother to Sam.'

'No, but he doesn't need me as much as he used to. I was starting to think about other things, getting my teaching certificate...' She blew out a breath. 'I don't know. I think I was starting to feel stymied. And maybe eventually Sam would, too.' She gazed at her son, who was drinking everything in. 'He's loving being here.'

'So far it has been nothing but a holiday,' Malik pointed out. 'But I hope he will welcome his place here, in time.'

The thought made Gracie's heart squeeze. 'When will you tell him?'

'Soon.' Malik paused. 'My grandfather told me yesterday that he has cancer.' His gaze rested on the melee in the square below. 'I believe he will only live a few months, if that.'

'I'm sorry,' Gracie said, and Malik sighed.

'There is no love lost between us.'

'But he is still the closest thing you have to a parent. No matter what, it is a loss.'

'Yes, that is true.'

She took a deep breath. 'So what does that mean for me? And for Sam?'

Malik turned back to look at her. 'Sam's position as my heir must be secured as soon as possible.'

'Secured?' A frisson of alarm skittered along Gracie's spine. 'How?'

Malik glanced at Sam and then back at her, his expression set. Gracie felt a stab of fear. He looked so *determined*. 'By being legitimised.'

'Legit— But how?' She didn't like to think of Sam as *illegitimate*. It was such a nasty word, a terrible concept. And yet for an heir to a throne, it was the unfortunate reality.

'How does any child become legitimate?' Malik asked in that implacable tone Gracie was starting to know well. 'By his parents marrying.'

The words fell into the stillness like stones into a pool, creating endless ripples. From the marketplace below someone let out a shout, and as if from a great distance Gracie heard a babble of Arabic. She refocused her stunned gaze on Malik.

'Are…are you serious?' she stammered.

'Never more so.'

Once again he'd completely shocked her, even as part of her acknowledged that she couldn't really be *that* surprised. Had some part of her wondered or, heaven help her, even hoped this would happen? That Malik would find a way for them to be together, and yet…

'What kind of marriage are you talking about?' She kept her voice low even though there was no way Sam could hear them. She could hardly believe she was asking the question. *Marriage.*

Malik hesitated, and that second's pause told her more than she'd ever wanted to know. 'A marriage based on convenience as well as respect and attraction.'

'Those are three totally different things.'

'Yet they can coexist.'

'Can they?' Gracie gazed out at the market square, trying to untangle the ferment of her feelings. *Marriage.* Was this what she wanted, a union based on expediency rather than any kind of love and affection? Because the message she was getting loud and clear was that Malik didn't love her. Never had and never would. And while her life in Illinois might have felt small, living in a loveless marriage felt even smaller. More constrictive and definitely more hopeless.

'It's not very romantic, is it?' she said after a moment, keeping her gaze on the market because she didn't want to see the expression in Malik's eyes.

'No, but I am not one for romance.'

'You were in Rome.' The champagne, the coins in the fountain, the fairy tale. What had happened to it all? Had he changed that much—or had he merely been presenting a front back then, as she'd feared?

'I am not that naïve boy any longer, Grace, and you are

not that girl. If you are looking for a fairy tale, you will not find it here.' Malik took a breath and then ploughed on. 'But in truth I do not think you will find it anywhere. What we could have would be much better. Much stronger. More real.'

'How?' The word emerged through numb lips. How was it possible to feel so hopeful and sad at the same time?

'Because the fairy tale fades away and notions of romantic love disappear. None of it is lasting or real.'

His unswerving belief in what he was saying made something wither inside her. 'Do you really believe that?'

'Yes.' Another pause as he deliberated what to say. She didn't know if she could take Malik running down the whole concept of love. Ten years of loneliness and, yes, she'd been holding out for the fairy tale. 'My father believed in the fairy tale,' Malik said. 'He thought he had it with my mother, and perhaps he did, although I do not know. But then she died and he never recovered. He walked away from his family, from his duty, from life, a weak and wrecked man. Is that the kind of life you really want?'

'No one wants to lose someone they love,' Gracie protested. 'I'm sorry for your father. He obviously experienced something very difficult.'

'And made it even more difficult. To be enslaved to emotion…to allow someone to have that power over you… who would want it?'

I would, Gracie thought. But not with someone who vowed never to feel the same. 'You obviously don't.'

'No.'

'And yet they say it's better to have loved and lost than never loved at all.' A flush rose to Gracie's cheeks. Did she love Malik? She could, she suspected, if she let herself, but how awful was it to think you could love someone who had no intention of loving you back? She sat back, not wanting to press the point.

'I do not share that sentiment.' Malik leaned forward, his eyes glittering. 'Gracie, when we marry, I will respect you with everything I am and have, treat you with kindness and honesty at all times, and make your body sing with pleasure every night. Surely those things are better than some ephemeral concept of *love*.'

He spoke the last word on a sneer that made Gracie blink. Her body felt warm. *Sing with pleasure every night.* Yes, she had no doubt Malik could do that—and the possibility of experiencing it at least once more was incredibly tempting. How could it not be? But it still didn't make up for the appalling lack—knowing someone would never return her feelings, never feel the intensity and devotion that she would feel. Living like that would be horrifying, soul-destroying. And yet that was what Malik was offering her.

'It's a big decision, Malik,' she said at last. 'I need some time to think.' Because she wasn't the only one involved in this. She had to think of Sam, too, and what was best for him.

'Of course,' Malik returned swiftly, but Gracie was just clocking that he'd said *when* they married, not if. Was the outcome really in question for him? *Did she have any choice?*

'Spend the next week getting to know Alazar,' Malik said. 'And getting to know me. And then you can make a decision, and we will discuss the matter again.'

Gracie nodded, accepting, even as she silently acknowledged that she didn't actually know what decision she was making—or if it had already been made for her.

The next week was surprisingly sweet. Although he still had to deal with matters of state, Malik found time to spend with both Gracie and Sam, whether it was merely relaxing by the pool or going further afield to see more of Alazar. He showed her the national park and the country's only zoo, with its camels, lemurs and a magnificent white tiger; they had meals in intimate rooms at the palace and picnics on a bluff overlooking the jewel-bright sea.

And they talked, sharing more than they ever had before, whether they were simple jokes or discussions of philosophy. Over the course of the week Malik felt as if the tightly held parts of himself were slowly loosening. He was enjoying things he'd never even considered before—the taste of good food, the beauty of a blue sky, the purity of his son's laughter. And spending time with Gracie, listening to her share her ideas.

He'd also enjoyed kissing her thoroughly at the end of each evening, although with effort he'd kept it to mere kisses. His body ached to do far more, and he knew Gracie's did, as well. But he hoped that an enforced abstinence might make Gracie more willing to agree to the marriage that would have to take place, and soon.

Every afternoon he spent an interminable half hour debriefing his grandfather, who was increasingly bedridden and twitching with impotent anger.

'You are making a fool of yourself with that woman. A fool,' he spat towards the end of the week. The gossip had finally reached his ears, although Malik had tried to be discreet.

'I am winning her over,' he stated calmly, suppressing the flash of rage his grandfather's contempt caused him. 'We cannot secure the succession without her, and a forced marriage will not help the kingdom. The days of such archaic arrangements are over.'

'Nonsense. Banish her to a remote palace—'

'This is the twenty-first century,' Malik cut him off.

'Do you think the Western world will do business with a country whose queen is in exile, simply because she is American?'

Asad glared at him and silently fumed. Malik knew his grandfather knew he was right—he just didn't want to admit it. 'I am wooing her gently,' he stated. 'It is necessary. If that makes me a fool in your eyes, then so be it. I will do what I must to secure my country's future as well as my throne.'

Sketching the briefest salaam, he turned on his heel and left the room.

Was he a fool? The question was like a fly buzzing about his brain as he returned to his private office, constantly annoying him. He'd spoken the truth to Asad, but only part of it.

He *was* enjoying his time with Gracie, necessary as it was. He was glad to get to know her as well as Sam, but he was conscious that he could not stay in such pleasant limbo for ever. He couldn't let himself weaken, or let his feelings for Gracie and Sam cloud his judgement. He needed to keep a distance between him and Gracie. He also needed to set a date for their wedding—but to do that he required Gracie's cooperation.

He found her on a bench in the gardens, a book opened on her lap, her face tilted to the sun.

'You look peaceful,' Malik remarked as he joined her on the bench.

A shy smile of pleasure lit her face and she closed her book. 'I *feel* peaceful, surprisingly.'

'Why surprisingly?'

'Because this is still all so strange, and I am very aware that the future is uncertain.' She eyed him, and Malik gave her a guarded smile.

'Where is Sam?'

'One of your staff took him to play boules. He's loving it here.'

'I am glad.'

'But this can't last for ever,' Gracie pointed out. 'In some ways it feels like the calm before a storm. I want life to go on like some endless holiday, but I know it can't.'

'No,' Malik agreed. 'It can't.' It was the perfect segue into talking about his own plans. 'I will need to make an announcement soon, about Sam.'

Gracie's eyes widened and her teeth sank deeper into her lip. 'Already?'

'Considering my grandfather's health, time is of the essence. I thought we could go away, the three of us, for a few nights. I want to show both of you the heart of Alazar. We can talk to Sam about who I am. Who he is.'

'That seems like a good idea,' Gracie agreed cautiously. 'But what happens after that?'

'I will announce Sam to my people.' He paused. 'After we have married.'

'Oh, really?' Her eyes flashed. 'What happened to me making a decision?'

'Gracie, you must see the inevitability of this. Sam cannot be my heir if he is not legitimate. I am trying to be as patient as I can, and I think we've both enjoyed this week together. But we must move ahead.' Asad's words echoed through him and he finished, his tone flat and final, 'We will marry as soon as we return from the mountains.'

'What a romantic proposal.'

'You know I am not romantic.'

'I also know I don't want to be bullied into a marriage,' Gracie snapped. 'You have to give me time, Malik—'

'I have given you time.'

'Without an actual choice! What is the point in that?'

Malik sighed, his patience at an end. 'What do you want me to do?'

'At least pretend I have some say in the matter,' Gracie answered sarcastically. 'Really, sometimes I wonder how much of your kindness is real and how much is an act simply to get what you want.' Her breath came out in a rush, her expression turning bleak. 'I don't know if I can live like that.'

Malik felt himself tense. In his impatience, he'd gone too fast, run too rough. 'We can be happy together, Gracie. I know we can.'

'Then wait and see if I come to the same conclusion,' Gracie answered quietly, her eyes still troubled. 'Can you at least give me that courtesy?'

Everything in Malik howled no. He wanted to make Sam his in the eyes of Alazar, but just as much he wanted to make Gracie his. But he knew enforcing his will now would backfire badly. 'Malik?' she prompted, her voice soft and sad. Wordlessly he nodded.

CHAPTER ELEVEN

'THERE IT IS.'

Malik leaned forward, one long, lean finger pointing out of the window of the helicopter towards the palace perched incongruously on a mountaintop. 'Palace of the Clouds.'

'Wow.' Gracie leaned forward as well, taking in the magnificent sight. The palace was a maze of rocky walls and tall towers, its foundations built directly onto the mountain, its turrets and minarets seeming to touch the sky. 'How on earth did they build it?'

'With much hard labour. It is eight hundred years old,' Malik said. 'Built by the Sultan for his favourite wife.'

Gracie arched an eyebrow. 'How many wives did he have?'

'I believe around six hundred.' Malik grinned. 'In that way, we have already moved forward.'

'What a relief.' The banter was light, but it still sent a frisson of alarmed awareness through her. She knew Malik was clinging to his patience for her to make a decision about their marriage. And really, it was no decision at all. She understood how little choice she had, and yet she needed to be sure in her own mind—and her own heart.

In some ways she felt as if she'd been moving inexorably towards this since Malik had appeared again in her life, but in another way... *Marriage. Being the wife of a sultan. Living in Alazar.* And more worrying…being married to a man who had as good as promised not to love her. Were the things Malik had said he could give her enough? Was she willing to relinquish any hope of loving and being loved for the sake of her son's legacy?

'Your father only had one wife, though, didn't he?' she remarked, remembering what he'd said earlier about his father living the fairy tale—the fairy tale he didn't want.

'Yes. As I said before, he only had one wife, and he loved her very much.'

There was a subtext to his words, to the cool tone he'd unconsciously adopted, and it was one Gracie didn't like— that Malik's father might have loved his wife, but Malik had no intention of loving his. She'd been trying to come to terms with that reality, but it was hard.

And yet in ten years she hadn't met a single man she'd been interested in dating, much less marrying. Maybe Malik's was her best offer, and in truth it was an attractive one. Respect, kindness, honesty, passion. These were all amazing things. So why did she still feel trepidation?

The answer was painfully obvious. Because she was falling in love with him. Because he'd hurt her once before, terribly, and after the week they'd spent together he now possessed immeasurably more power to hurt her again, and far worse. Was what he was offering worth that risk? Could she live in a marriage knowing her love wasn't returned and never would be?

'Where does the helicopter land?' she asked as she looked out of the window to avoid Malik's direct gaze as well as the unhappy circling of her own thoughts.

'There is a helipad behind the palace, on a flat outcropping of rock.'

'That's convenient.'

'Not at all. It was blasted several years ago, when my

grandfather wished the Palace of the Clouds to be more accessible. Before the helipad, it would have taken a seven-day trek on camel to get here.'

'Now, that would have been cool,' Sam said, and Malik and Gracie exchanged a wry smile. Moments later they were landing, and then a member of staff was escorting them across the rocky terrain to a steep set of stairs cut directly into the mountainside that led to the palace's main entrance.

Gracie stopped to admire the view—an endless, snow-capped mountain range with the desert beyond. The bleakness she'd once seen from the royal jet now held undeniable beauty.

'I can't believe anyone made it up here, much less built a palace,' she said. Malik took her elbow to help her up the stairs.

'I told you, I come from a strong and independent people.'

'So does your son,' Gracie murmured, for Sam had strode ahead, taking the steps two at a time despite their precarious placement.

'He will make a good sultan.'

Gracie didn't reply; the prospect of her son being leader of a country still sent her nerves jangling.

Malik took her hand and squeezed it. 'It will be all right, Gracie,' he murmured.

'You sound very sure.'

'I am sure.'

She glanced at him, wishing she could understand what was going on behind that opaque gaze, that unreadable expression. The last week had been wonderful, but it hadn't always felt real. Their marriage wouldn't be an extended holiday, and they wouldn't even have the prospect of more children to look forward to, a fact that Gracie thought she could come to terms with but still found sorrowful. She would have liked to have a little girl with Malik's dark hair and sudden smile.

But far beyond that, she would have liked to have Malik's love. At times, when he was laughing with Sam or talking with her, she felt as if she could glimpse, momentarily, that hidden part of him. The man beneath the cold, autocratic exterior, the boy he'd once been. He was still there, in those little glimpses, but was that enough? Was any of this enough or was she about to embark on a lifetime of loneliness and heartache?

Inside, the palace was surprisingly airy and light. Refreshments had been laid out in a salon, and the three of them ate together, relaxing after the helicopter ride, until Sam was once again racing off, eager to explore.

'Let me show you the delights of the palace,' Malik entreated, and took Gracie by the hand as they went after Sam.

The palace was as luxurious as the one in Teruk, with large rooms gilded in gold and jewels and amazing views from every window. Gracie didn't think she'd ever tire of the sight of the snowy mountains thrusting proudly up to an achingly blue sky.

'But I must show you the palace's *pièce de résistance*,' Malik said with a teasing smile, and he ushered Sam and Gracie to a set of double doors that led to the most incredible sight Gracie had ever seen.

'Wow,' Sam breathed, and Gracie could only echo him. 'Wow. Is that…?'

'A natural waterfall, yes.'

The back of the palace had been built right into the mountain rock, and a natural waterfall poured into a set of swimming pools laid out on terraces, cascading into one another.

'The water must be freezing,' Gracie said, and Malik smiled.

'The pools are heated.'

They spent the next few hours swimming and relaxing by the pool, as any family might, and Gracie felt as if her heart were teetering, one moment filled with hope and happiness and then the next clenched in fear. She was afraid to want this too much. To hope too much, and for something that Malik had told her would never happen.

Sam dared them both to stand under the icy waterfall, and, laughing, Gracie did so, shrieking as the freezing water fell about her. Then Malik grabbed her hand and pulled her out of the waterfall, to the other side, so the cascading water was a curtain shielding them from the world.

Gracie looked around her in amazement; they were in a secret, rocky chamber, the roar of the waterfall the only sound. Then she caught sight of the look of blazing need in Malik's eyes and any appreciation of her surroundings fell away in light of that shining certainty.

'I want you,' he growled. 'So much I can hardly bear it.'

Her heart rate tripped. 'But you've barely touched me all week…'

'And it just about killed me.' Already he was pulling her towards him, her slick body sliding against his in a way that felt unbearably erotic.

'Why did you stay away, then?' Gracie breathed. Malik's hands were everywhere, and yet she still couldn't get enough.

'Because I wanted our wedding night to be all the sweeter. But now I don't think I can wait.' And then his mouth was on hers, his tongue plundering its depths, his body thrusting against hers with delicious intent.

Gracie sagged against the rock wall, helpless under Malik's wonderful onslaught. One hand nudged aside her swimming costume, his fingers teasing the very centre of her so it felt as if lightning were racing through her veins, to accompany the thundering of her heart.

Her nails bit into his arm as the overwhelming sensations cascaded through her, both sizzling and sweet.

'Malik,' she gasped out as his fingers moved even more intimately against her. Her hips rocked against his hand. *'Malik...'*

'Mom!' Sam's voice came to them from beyond the protective wall of water. 'Are you guys lost in there?'

Yes, she was lost. And losing more of herself with every passing second. With a groan Gracie pulled away from Malik. 'You can't leave me like this.'

The smile he gave her was full of sensual promise. 'What if I make it up to you later?'

She thrilled at his words, her body coming alive again just at the thought. 'Do you mean that?'

'I can't last much longer without you,' Malik admitted in a low voice. 'I want you too much, Gracie.'

Sam called again and reluctantly Gracie moved away from Malik. 'I should go back to our son.'

Malik's face softened. 'I like hearing you say that.'

'Say what?'

'Our son. Not yours. Not mine. *Ours.*'

His gaze held hers and Gracie's heart started to beat hard again. Yes, Sam was theirs. She felt their shared responsibility, their partnership, more than ever now—for better or for worse. And she knew in that moment she would marry him—that she would fall into this adventure because it was the one she wanted. *He* was the one she wanted. She loved him, and she dared to hope that one day he might learn to love her back.

'Tonight,' Malik promised, his voice rough with longing, and Gracie nodded.

'Tonight.'

'What were you doing?' Sam demanded as Gracie emerged from behind the waterfall, her heart still skittering around from her encounter with Malik.

'There's a little cave back there,' Gracie said, and thankfully her voice sounded normal. 'Malik showed it to me. You should see it.'

'A cave? Cool!' Sam dived under the water and Gracie sank onto the ledge of the pool. She needed a moment to recover. Her whole body was trembling with the aftershocks of Malik's sure touch. She felt as if she might dissolve, trickle right into the pool in a puddle of need. She couldn't wait for nightfall.

From behind the waterfall she could hear Sam's excited shout and the low rumble of Malik's response. A few minutes later they emerged, dripping wet and grinning. Gracie didn't think she'd ever tire of the sight of Malik in swimming trunks. His chest was a thing of glorious beauty, perfectly sculpted muscles tapering to narrow hips and powerful thighs. Malik caught her look and gave her an admonishing look back.

'Keep looking at me like that and I will embarrass myself and you,' he muttered as he passed by her, and Gracie couldn't keep from grinning.

A greedy sense of expectation had her practically dancing on her tiptoes all evening, as the three of them ate dinner in one of the palace's more intimate dining rooms. Every secret, sliding look, every brush of Malik's fingers had her whole body tingling in yearning response.

The mood of anticipation continued as she tucked Sam into bed and then retired to her sumptuous bedroom down the hall. There was no harem in this remote palace, just a lovely room, the double bed on its own dais, the windows overlooking the stunning alpine vista.

Gracie took a bath and then slipped into the one semi-sexy nightgown that she owned, a simple white silk sheath with lace straps. She'd bought it on a whim and never worn it—now she laughed at herself for bringing it to Alazar at all. Had she known this would happen? Had she *hoped*?

And here she was, still hoping. It was ten o'clock at night and Malik still hadn't come. Should she go find him? Dared she?

As she was summoning up the courage to do just that, a soft knock sounded on the door. Gracie stilled, anchored to the floor. Another soft knock, and then she flew to the door and opened it.

Malik stood there, looking devastatingly sexy in an off-white linen shirt open at the throat and a pair of loose trousers. His hair was slightly rumpled as if he'd run his hands through it and his mouth curved in a smile of deep appreciation, his eyes lightening to silver as his gaze flicked over Gracie.

Suddenly she felt conscious of how little she was wearing. The cream silk was thin, and he could probably see just about everything, including her body's immediate response to his presence.

'I was hoping you'd come,' she said huskily, and his eyes flashed fire.

'I was hoping you'd say that.'

Wordlessly her heart seeming to fling itself against her ribs, she stepped aside. Malik came into the room and shut the door behind him.

'You're sure?' he asked quietly, his gaze steady on her, and Gracie let out a laugh that was half wild.

'Am I sure? I've been wearing grooves in the floor, pacing, wondering if I should go and find *you*.'

'That answers my question, then,' Malik murmured, and then he came towards her. 'We'll have our wedding night a little early.' He paused. 'Assuming you have made a decision…?'

'Was there any decision to make?'

'You asked me to give you time, Gracie.'

'I know.' She swallowed hard, excitement and trepidation surging within her. She felt as if she were on the edge of a precipice, about to take that nerve-jangling step into the utter unknown. 'I don't need any more time, Malik. I've made my decision.' She took a deep breath. 'I will marry you.'

'Then you have made me very happy.' The words ended on a shudder as Malik slid his hands from her shoulders to her waist. His palms fitted perfectly, his fingers splayed over her hips. Gently he drew her towards him.

'We are going to have a good life together, Gracie,' he whispered, and brushed a kiss across her lips.

Gracie let out a breathy laugh. 'I don't know why I feel so nervous.'

He brushed a tendril of hair away from her face, his fingers skimming her cheek. 'There's no need to be nervous.'

'I know. But…' She hesitated, then continued with a flush, 'it's been a long time for me.'

'And me, too.'

Somehow she didn't think Malik had been celibate for ten years. 'I mean, a *really* long time.'

His gentle smile morphed into a frown of puzzlement. 'Do you mean…?'

Gracie nodded. 'You've been my only lover, Malik.' Before he could say anything, she rushed on, 'I know I haven't been yours. I'm not asking…'

'There haven't been that many. A handful of meaningless exchanges,' Malik murmured. 'And trust me, no one has come close to you, Gracie.'

'Okay,' she mumbled. Her face felt fiery. He took her fingers and kissed them.

'But I don't want to talk about any of that,' he said, and with a little smile he nibbled on the tips of her fingers. 'In fact, I'm not sure I want to talk at all.'

'Sounds good to me.' If they talked any more, she might really put her foot in it. She might, caught up in the moment, admit she was falling in love with him, and she couldn't bear to see the appalled look in Malik's eyes when he heard that revelation. No, she'd keep that particular news to herself, at least for now, and hope that one day he might want to hear those words.

Malik drew her to him again and kissed her softly, like a question. Gracie answered by parting her lips, letting his tongue sweep inside. The second kiss was deeper, seeming to plunge right inside her. And then she stopped counting because the kisses were merging into one another, melting her insides.

Malik backed her towards the bed, laughing softly as he gently tipped her onto it and then came to lie down next to her.

'Do you remember…?' he began, and Gracie nodded, for the memories were sweeping through her, colliding with the present in the most achingly emotional way.

'Yes, I remember everything. Every moment, every touch.'

'So do I,' Malik whispered, and kissed her again. 'I remember how soft your skin felt,' he said as he slid the straps of her nightgown from her shoulders. 'I remember how perfect your breasts were. And still are,' he added as he slid the nightgown to her waist, and kissed each rosy tip. Gracie let out a shudder of longing. 'I remember how you liked this,' Malik murmured, taking his time, lavishing attention on her body in a way that made Gracie writhe in need. 'I remember how you responded. You were so untouched.' He lifted his head to look at her with glittering eyes. 'And so was I. You were my first, Gracie. My first everything.' He pressed a kiss to her stomach and then moved lower. 'My first and my last,' he said, and Gracie gasped both from his words and the touch of his mouth at her centre.

Her hips arched up helplessly as she pressed her head back against the pillow, awash in sensation, drowning in pleasure.

Her fingernails dug into his shoulders as the intense pleasure she was feeling tightened into an aching, ascending point that peaked as she let out a cry, her body relaxing as the waves rippled through her.

'And that's just the beginning,' Malik promised. Gracie laughed shakily.

'I'm not sure I can take much more.'

'Oh, trust me, you can. I'll make sure of it.' He lay braced on his forearms, his gaze fastened on her. 'Touch me, Gracie.'

The plea reached right inside her and with a shy smile she skimmed her hands down the hard planes of his chest, her fingers exploring the ridge of the scar on his torso.

'Where did you get this?'

'An assassination attempted by a member of a hostile tribe.'

'Assassination…' Gracie withdrew her hand as she stared at him in appalled surprise. 'I didn't realise it was that dangerous.'

'It isn't any more. And that man wasn't in his right mind.' Malik reached for her hand and drew it back to him. 'And I'm not in *my* right mind, not until you start touching me again.'

Laughing softly, Gracie glided her hand down his chest and thigh before she wrapped her fingers around his arousal, amazed at the sheer power and strength of him. He was so beautiful, so male, and he was hers. She stroked him gently, her fingers playing with the hot, silky length of him, as Malik's breath hissed between his teeth.

'That feels *very* good.'

'It's been so long,' Gracie whispered. She found it hard to believe that she could affect him so powerfully. 'And I have so little experience...'

'Your touch lights me up like no other, Gracie. I promise you that.'

The idea that she affected him more than anyone else was heady. Gracie's strokes became bolder and more daring until Malik rolled her over onto her back, poised above her, his erection nudging her thighs.

'What about protection?' she whispered, and his mouth twisted.

'We don't need any.'

Realisation slammed into her. 'I'm sorry...'

'Don't be.' He kissed her hard on the mouth. 'You are all I want, Gracie. All I need.'

'You're all I need, Malik,' she returned on a gasp as he slid inside her, filling her up, making her shudder with both the strangeness and rightness of it.

She wrapped her legs around his waist as they began to move in rhythm, finding it instinctively, reaching for that release yet again, their bodies straining and searching.

'Malik...' Gracie gasped, and then she couldn't manage any more for she was climbing, climbing, and then it felt as if fireworks went off inside her as they reached the

peak together, Malik burying his head in her neck as his body shuddered.

Afterwards Gracie was conscious of the sudden quiet, her thudding heart. Malik was still inside her as he kissed her collarbone and then her lips, and then gently rolled off her. Gracie felt the loss, but that momentary pang was quelled when Malik turned to smile at her, reaching for her hand.

They lay there quietly, fingers interlaced and resting on top of Gracie's belly. The only sound was their own breathing.

As her heart rate slowed and her heated skin cooled, Gracie wondered what had just happened. What it meant. How much it meant. She was aware, more than ever, that Malik had made no promises. Maybe he'd just stick her in the harem and visit her when he felt like it. Maybe that was what marriage looked like in Alazar, even in the twenty-first century.

'Stop.' Malik squeezed her hand and Gracie glanced over at him, startled.

'What?'

'I can see that your mind is already starting to race. You don't need to fear, Gracie. I told you that before.'

She blushed, embarrassed that her thoughts had been so easy for him to read. Malik smiled and kissed her before putting his arm around her and pulling her against him.

'So you've promised me this every night?' she dared to tease, and Malik laughed softly.

'Absolutely.'

'And what about the days? What will those look like?'

'How do you want them to look?'

Gracie considered. 'I don't want to be stuck in the palace all day, or treated like some ornament.'

'Of course not.'

'I'd like to work, or at least devote myself to good causes. Help with education for girls and those with special needs...'

'That all sounds wonderful to me. You can be an amazing asset to this country, Gracie. You can join with me to bring it into a new and modern age.'

'Partners,' Gracie suggested, and Malik nodded.

'Yes. Partners.'

She snuggled against him, breathing a sigh of both contentment and relief. It wasn't love, but maybe it would be one day. And for now she would choose to be happy.

CHAPTER TWELVE

DAZZLING SUNLIGHT WOKE Gracie the next morning. The bed next to her was empty, and she felt a pang of loss. It didn't last long, though, for the day was too fresh and beautiful to spend a moment moping. She felt energised and excited for what lay ahead, more than she could ever remember feeling before. Partners, Malik had said. The anxiety she'd been wrestling with for weeks was finally falling away.

She rose from the bed and went to the window, kneeling on the window seat of ancient, weathered stone as she gazed out at the breathtaking view, rugged peaks and undulating desert underneath a brilliant blue sky.

'What are you smiling about?' Malik came into the bedroom, smiling himself, dressed casually in jeans and a cotton shirt.

'Everything,' Gracie admitted. 'I feel very happy this morning.'

'As do I.' He reached for her and she came easily, wrapping her arms around his waist as she rested her cheek against his chest, felt the steady thud of his heart beneath her. 'Is Sam awake?'

'Yes, I just had breakfast with him and he's now gone to the pool. One of my staff is watching him.'

'He's had the time of his life here.'

'Yes.' Malik's arms tightened around her. 'I thought we could talk to him today. Tell him who I really am.'

Gracie's heart lurched a little, but she knew it was time. It felt right. 'Okay.'

'I've arranged for us to go pony trekking through the mountains. It will hopefully be enjoyable for all of us, and it will afford us the privacy to tell Sam.' He paused. 'Things will be set in motion quickly afterwards, Gracie. I want you to be prepared for that.'

Gracie let out a shaky laugh. 'I'm not sure there's any way to be prepared for that. But I need to make my own arrangements, Malik.' She eased herself away from his embrace so she could look up at him. 'I want to call my parents, and I'd like my family to come to the wedding.' Malik hesitated, and Gracie frowned. 'Is that a problem?'

'Not necessarily, but our marriage will have to be as soon as possible after our return so no one can challenge Sam's rights. There won't be time for your family to attend.'

'Couldn't we wait a few days?'

'Time is of the essence.' Malik hesitated. 'But if it is really important, perhaps we could manage something.'

'Do you mean that?' Gracie was touched that he was so concerned about her wishes.

'Yes, of course. The other option is we could have a formal reception and celebration in a week or two. Your parents and family could come then.'

Gracie nodded slowly. If Malik could compromise, then she could, too. 'Okay, that sounds like a plan.' Smiling, he kissed her.

An hour later they were setting off through the mountains on ponies, with Gracie clutching the reins of hers rather tightly.

'I've never actually been horseback riding before,' she confessed to Malik, and he gave her a reassuring grin.

'These animals are very gentle.'

Still, after an hour Gracie was glad to slide off and wobble towards the stream where the ponies were being led to for a drink.

'Thank goodness for the helipad,' she said as she rubbed her legs. 'Seven days by camel would have just about killed me.'

'You will need to get a little hardier, I think,' Malik said with a smile as he took her by the hand and drew her down to the blanket several servants had spread out. A picnic was already being unpacked, dishes of dates and figs, meats and cheeses spread out for their consumption.

'I don't know,' Gracie said, plucking a fig from its bowl. 'Life in Alazar seems pretty luxurious. I think I'll get used to the five-star-hotel treatment pretty quickly. In fact, I already have.'

'I'm glad to hear it.'

'It's going to be hard for you to go back home,' Sam teased as he joined them on the blanket. 'Back to making supper and washing dishes!' As Sam reached for a date, Malik and Gracie exchanged looks.

'Actually, Sam,' Malik said, his voice friendly and mild, 'what would you think about staying in Alazar for longer?'

'Longer?' Sam looked up, chewing the date, his gaze narrowed. He swallowed and asked, 'What do you mean?'

Gracie held her breath, waiting, wondering how Malik would explain this. How Sam would respond.

'I mean,' Malik said carefully, 'what would you think about living in Alazar?'

'Living…' Sam stared at him blankly. Then he looked at Gracie, a hint of hurt confusion in his eyes. 'Are you thinking about moving?'

'Well, yes,' Gracie said. 'Maybe. That is…' She looked helplessly at Malik.

'You came to Alazar for a reason, Sam,' he said, his voice quiet and strong and sure. 'Not just for a holiday, or because I am your mother's friend. In fact, I am more than her friend. Your mother and I intend to marry.' Malik kept Sam's gaze unwaveringly while Sam stared back at him, his mind racing.

'You mean…you…you'd be like my dad?' Hope and uncertainty were both audible in his voice.

'Yes, I would. In fact, I wouldn't be *like* your dad.' Malik smiled, and the hint of vulnerability in his expression made Gracie ache. 'I *am* your father, Sam.'

'What…?' Sam's breath came out in a rush. 'How?' He gave Gracie another look full of confusion. 'Mom said she'd never been able to get in touch with my father.'

'She wasn't. And I didn't know about you until very recently. If I had, I would have been part of your life. A big part. I promise.' Sincerity throbbed in Malik's voice and Gracie had to blink back sudden tears. She didn't doubt for a second that Malik cared for his son very much.

Sam stared down at the blanket, his brow furrowed, his mouth working, as he processed so much. Gracie put a hand on his thin shoulder and squeezed.

'But you're Sultan,' Sam finally said, looking up. Malik nodded, waiting for more. 'What does that mean for me?' Trust Sam to make that leap almost instantly. Her son was fiercely intelligent.

'It means you'd be Sultan after me.'

'Sultan…' Sam looked away.

'How do you feel about that, Sam?' Malik asked quietly.

Sam kicked at the dirt. 'I don't know.'

'It is a lot to take in, I understand. Nothing needs to change right now.'

'But it has changed,' Sam said, a note of accusation entering his voice. 'Will I even get to go back to Illinois? To my home?'

'Of course you will,' Malik answered steadily. 'For visits.'

'I didn't mean *visits*,' Sam retorted. He looked up, his eyes bright with both anger and tears. 'Why are you telling me all this now? Why did you *lie* to me all along? I hate you!' He threw Malik a vicious look, and then he scrambled up from the blanket and stalked away. Gracie half rose to go after him, but Malik stayed her with one hand.

'Let him go. My staff will keep an eye on him and he needs some time alone.' His face was impassive, his tone quiet, but Gracie sensed his hurt. He had wanted his son to embrace him and all he'd offered, and he hadn't.

'He didn't mean it,' Gracie said, and Malik did not reply. She tried again. 'This isn't a rejection of you, Malik. He just needs some time.'

He managed a stiff smile that didn't reach his eyes. 'I know.'

They ate in silence, conscious of Sam sloping about the rocks a few dozen metres away, his head bent, his shoulders hunched. Gracie ached to comfort both Malik and Sam, to draw this unconventional family together and make it stronger than ever before.

Glancing sideways at Malik, she thought about his refusal to love, that ephemeral notion he disdained because it had made his father weak. But was Malik afraid of being weak—or being hurt? How could she convince him it was worth the risk?

They were all still subdued as they packed up the lunch and got back on the ponies. Half an hour of trekking later, Malik pulled his pony over by a rocky overhang. Gracie and Sam followed suit, and he gestured to them to follow him into the shallow cave.

'This is where my ancestor Sultan Raji al Bahjat camped when he was being attacked by the Ottomans,' he told them quietly. 'He led his people to an overwhelming victory despite the huge odds against him.' Malik placed a hand on Sam's shoulder. 'He was a wonderful leader. He was your ancestor as well as mine.'

Sam didn't say anything, and Gracie perched on a rock, her knees drawn up to her chest, her heart in her mouth.

'You are his descendant, Sam,' Malik stated quietly. 'You have the blood of sultans and kings running through your veins. Alazar itself is in your blood.' Malik scooped up a handful of crumbly, pebbly soil and pressed it into Sam's hand. 'You may fight against it now, because it is strange and even unwelcome, but it is the truth.'

Sam stared at Malik for a long moment, and then he opened his hand so the soil spilled out, showering their feet. 'I want to go home,' he said quietly, then turned and walked from the cave.

Gracie stood up, her heart beating painfully. 'Malik...' she began, but he just shook his head and brushed by her.

They rode in silence back to the Palace of the Clouds, and Sam and Malik both disappeared once inside to their own pursuits, leaving Gracie feeling lonely and heartsick. She wanted Malik to reassure her that everything was going to be okay, even as she craved to reassure him. He was hurting, and he was choosing not to let her close. Both of her men were. In the end she called her parents to have a conversation that was long overdue.

'You're staying in Alazar?' Her mother sounded appalled and incredulous once she'd explained she was to marry Malik.

'Yes, although of course we'll come back to visit. But

Sam belongs here, Mom, and so do I.' *I think.* She closed her eyes, battling against the uncertainty that was crashing over her in waves. She realised afresh how fragile everything was, for her to feel this way now. The anxiety that had fallen away this morning was coming back in full force.

'But the Middle East…it's so far away…'

'Malik has promised you can visit any time. And we'll visit you. In fact, we're planning a wedding reception in a couple of weeks. I'd love it if all of you could come.'

'Of course we'll come, Gracie,' her dad said. 'We wouldn't miss it for the world.' The warmth in his voice made Gracie's eyes sting. She'd needed that reassurance.

Sam stayed in his room for dinner, and Gracie and Malik ate alone. She tried to engage him, alternating between stilted offers of reassurance and attempts at teasing banter, but it all fell flat.

'I'm sorry,' Malik said as a servant cleared away their dishes. He rubbed his temples, looking more tired and careworn than Gracie had ever seen him before. 'I have been distracted tonight, and not just by Sam. There are issues of state that concern me, as always.'

'I'm sorry,' Gracie said, knowing the words were inadequate. 'Is there anything I can do to help?'

Malik shook his head. 'No, but we should return to Teruk sooner than I had hoped.'

Gracie went to bed alone, aching for Malik, but he'd said he needed to work. Was this a vision of the future? Gracie wondered as she hugged a pillow to herself. Nights alone, a distant husband and an embittered and angry son? At that moment everything felt like a huge and disastrous mistake.

She dozed off eventually, only to wake when she felt Malik slide into bed next to her. Sleepily she turned to him, surprise flooding through her when he pulled her almost roughly into his arms and buried his face in her neck.

'Malik...'

'I need you, Gracie.' He kissed her hard, his hands roving over her body, sliding under her nightgown, every movement urgent and demanding, a plea Gracie understood. She hadn't been able to reassure him earlier, but she could now, and her body was responding in kind, craving the comfort as well as the exquisite release she knew their union would bring.

'Please...' Malik gasped. 'Touch me. I need you to touch me. I need to feel you...'

'Oh, Malik.' Tears stung her eyes as she pressed her lips to his chest. Malik groaned as she kissed her way down his body, offering him her body in return, her heart and soul, every touch of her lips her way of telling him she loved him. And his acceptance of her gift, his admission of how he needed her, was his way of saying it back. She had to believe that. She *did* believe that.

'Gracie...' Malik's hands were on her shoulders, his body arching instinctively as her mouth moved lower against his abdomen, his erection pushing against her. She hesitated, because she'd never done this before, but she wanted to show Malik how much she loved him. How much she was giving him, offering him her entire self, everything she had and was and could be, in that moment and for ever.

His breath came out in a hiss as she moved lower and then took him into her mouth. His hands tangled in her hair and Gracie revelled in the selfless act of love she was offering.

He came with a loud cry, his body shuddering before he pulled her up towards him, flipping her on her back as he drove deeply inside her. Gracie wrapped her legs around his waist, the sensation so sudden and overwhelming and intrinsically right that she gasped aloud.

Malik pressed his forehead against hers as he moved inside her and she matched his rhythm. 'I'm not hurting you?'

'No,' she assured him. She arched upwards, drawing him even deeper into herself, taking everything from him and giving it all back. '*No.* You could never hurt me, Malik.' *I love you,* she almost said. The words were on her lips, in her heart, bubbling up, demanding to be spoken. She bit them back at the last minute, overcome by the pleasure of their united bodies as they moved in sensuous rhythm, bodies straining, mouths gasping, hands seeking, until a climax crashed over them that shook Gracie right down to her marrow, reverberating through her bones and leaving her weak and utterly sated.

Afterwards Malik held on to her, rolling onto his back so Gracie lay sprawled over him, their bodies still wrapped around one another so Gracie didn't know where she left off and he began. Malik buried his face in her hair, and she felt his body shuddering, his arms clasped tightly around her. Neither of them spoke; neither of them needed to. In that moment their communication felt silent, perfect and pure. *I love you* didn't even need to be said.

'It won't be long.'

Malik gazed at his grandfather's face in the satellite video call and felt a strange plunging sensation in his middle. 'What do you mean?' he asked, even though he had a feeling he knew exactly what Asad meant.

'I'm dying,' Asad said bluntly. 'And the cancer is quicker than anyone anticipated. I have weeks, maybe a month, no longer.' He closed his eyes, shuddering as a pain gripped him, his face pale and waxy. Then he opened them once more and stared bleakly at Malik. 'There is much to say and little time to say it.'

'Say what you will,' Malik answered. His voice was terse, his chest tight with emotion he couldn't quite identify. He'd been feeling far too much these last few days— first with Sam's apparent rejection of him, and then last night with Gracie, their passion more intense, more emotional, than anything he'd ever experienced. Remembering it filled him with a mixture of joy and shame; he'd revealed so much weakness, showed her how much he needed her, and yet it had felt so good. So *right*.

'I have had time to reflect, these last weeks and months,' Asad said slowly. 'And I fear I have, over the years, been too harsh with you.'

For a moment Malik could not form words to reply. Too harsh? He thought of the cruel words, the beatings, the taunts, the enforced regime. Yes, his grandfather had been too harsh. And it was too late for regrets or even forgiveness.

'I feared for Alazar,' Asad continued. 'Its stability is more crucial than ever in this current climate of war and extremism. I wanted to safeguard it, and perhaps you have paid the price.' He sighed heavily. 'As did Azim.'

'Well I know it.'

'I was afraid for you,' his grandfather explained. His words came slowly, his face haggard with the effort. 'Afraid you would turn out like your father.'

'I hope I have not disappointed you too much,' Malik said stiffly.

'No, but I still fear,' Asad answered. 'With this woman… do not make the mistake your father made, Malik, and love a woman the way he did. It made him weak, even frail. He never would have been a good ruler of our people. He cared too much, and he lost all when your mother died. Do not be the same, and cause the ruin not only of your own country, but your own soul. Love is weakness, Malik. I have always told you that, and I have seen it proved right.'

Malik kept his face neutral as he absorbed his grandfather's words. He'd come from Gracie's bed only hours ago, and he could still smell her scent on him, remember how much weakness he'd shown last night when he'd reached for her. *I need you, Gracie.* He cringed now at the admission he'd made in a moment of desperation.

'I am not in love with her.' The words came out flat, cold. He meant them. At least, he wanted to mean them. He needed to mean them, because, as Asad had said, love was weakness. He'd known that, seen it in the way his father had lost his reason for living when his mother had died. Felt it in himself, when he'd realised how much power Gracie had. Needing her, feeling less than whole without her.

The last week had been a dream of sunshine and happiness, not reality. The reality was a marriage of convenience, a life of duty and a great deal of hard work. Not something as nebulous and untrustworthy as *love*.

'Good.' Asad nodded slowly; Malik could see he was tiring. 'Then marry her and keep her where you must. And return home quickly if you can.'

'We will leave today.'

After the call, Malik remained in his bedroom, his unseeing gaze on the distant snow-capped mountains. A few birds twittered their early-morning song, but otherwise the entire palace was hushed and still. *Now what?*

Now, he knew, he would have to go ahead with his plans. Marry Gracie in a quiet civil ceremony, and announce Sam to the world. He hated the thought of his son resisting such a move, but he knew he had no choice. News of Asad's illness had already leaked to the press. The vultures would soon start circling.

* * *

'What's wrong?'

Gracie gazed at Malik's serious expression and felt her insides plunge. She'd been looking forward to seeing him again, after their intense encounter last night. Now, as he stood in the doorway of her bedroom, a deep frown marring the sculpted perfection of his features, dread took over. 'What's happened?'

'My grandfather has taken a turn for the worse,' Malik said after a pause. 'He is dying, and the end will come sooner than anyone thought.'

'I'm so sorry, Malik.' Relief coursed through her at the realisation that she wasn't causing that frown, but it was edged with concern for this man she knew she loved. 'Do you want to return to Teruk?'

'Yes, we will have to leave this afternoon.' Malik passed a hand over his face. 'Everything will happen quickly now.'

'I understand.' She wished she felt more ready. She wished she felt closer to Malik, for despite their amazing intimacy last night he was the cold and distant stranger again this morning. When he looked as inscrutable as this, she had no idea how to reach him, or even if she could. And yet they were soon to be married.

An hour later they were boarding the helicopter, and, although he was quiet, Sam's simmering resentment seemed to have run its course, and Gracie was glad for that. Her son would get used to this new life and relish the challenges and opportunities. She only wished she felt more confident in herself, secure in Malik's feelings for her— whatever those were.

Last night, when he'd pulled her to him with such desperate urgency, she'd wondered if he loved her already, but simply didn't have the words for it. Last night his body had told her he loved her, but now Gracie wondered if that was just so much wishful thinking, because she wanted Malik's love so much.

Now, in the bright, harsh light of day, all her uncertainties had come rushing back. She longed for Malik to turn to her with a reassuring smile, to squeeze her hand. She craved his strength for everything that lay ahead, but Malik was completely cut off from her, silent and stony-faced. He didn't even look at her once.

Her stomach seethed with nerves as the flat-roofed buildings of Teruk came in view as the helicopter started its descent, the sky above turning lavender. Gracie caught Sam's eye and he gave her a lopsided smile.

'It's going to be okay, Mom.'

Gracie managed a smile back, humbled by her son's strength. He would, she realised, make a very good leader.

Back at the palace Malik disappeared into an office and Gracie was shepherded back to the harem. The rooms that had felt like a luxurious hotel days ago now felt like a gilded prison. Was Malik going to make the announcement? Shouldn't she be briefed? And when on earth were they going to get married?

She paced the living room of the suite, longing for answers and even more for Malik. For his solid, steadying presence, his sense of unshakeable strength, his sudden, brilliant smile. She *needed* him.

A sudden whirring of helicopter blades had her hurrying towards the window. Gracie watched as another helicopter touched down, wondering what important person had arrived at the palace.

She found out after an hour more of restless pacing, when the same servant woman who had attended to her on the first day arrived with a dinner tray.

'Thank you,' Gracie murmured as she took the tray. 'Do you know who arrived by helicopter about an hour ago?'

'Yes, it is the most amazing thing! A true miracle.' The woman shook her head, her eyes wide and round.

'Yes?' Gracie prompted, a touch of impatience in her voice, trepidation starting its relentless creep.

'It is His Highness's brother, who was lost twenty years ago now,' the woman said. 'It is His Highness Azim, the heir to the throne, returned to take his rightful place.'

CHAPTER THIRTEEN

MALIK STARED AT the man with the dark hair and menacing face, dressed in an expertly cut Italian suit. It had been twenty years since Malik had seen him last, but he had no doubts. He was looking at his brother, Azim.

Azim stopped in front of him, his face unsmiling, his features looking as if they'd been hewn from stone. A scar, a line of puckered red flesh, snaked from the corner of his eye to the cleft of his chin. The servant who had ushered him in stepped back, closing the doors of the salon and leaving the two brothers alone.

'Azim,' Malik said again. He wanted to embrace his brother, but he felt as if he were moving underwater; it was hard to breathe. Azim did not move or speak at all. 'What happened to you?' he asked hoarsely. 'Why are you here?'

'Not much of a welcome, then,' Azim replied. His voice was low and cynical, with the hint of a sneer. Malik recoiled at the implication.

'Of course I welcome you. *Of course.* I am just so surprised. Azim…we took you for dead. There was no ransom note, no demands all those years ago…' Malik shook his head, his mind reeling. He'd spent the last few hours drafting an announcement to the people of Alazar regarding his marriage to Gracie and Sam's place as his heir. He'd been so consumed with the task that he'd barely registered the helicopter's landing, had been surprised to be interrupted by a servant, who had told him he had a visitor. His brother.

'I was dead,' Azim returned flatly. 'But I am alive again, and I have returned.'

'I am so glad—'

'Are you?' Azim asked cynically, and Malik stared at him, trying to understand the undercurrents. And then he realised.

'You will be Sultan,' he said slowly. 'That is why you have come.'

'Will you challenge my inheritance?'

Malik lifted his chin, his eyes flashing. 'I am not a usurper.'

Azim's expression relaxed a little. 'I am pleased to hear it.'

It felt like too much to think about all at once. 'Please, sit down,' Malik said. 'I will ring for refreshments. Clearly we have much to talk about.'

Azim nodded tersely and they both sat down on a pair of settees by the window. Malik called for mint tea and a servant scurried to do his bidding, leaving them alone once more.

He gazed at Azim, noting the hardness in his mouth and eyes, the way he sat alert and ready, as if for an imminent attack. 'Where have you been all these years?' he asked quietly.

Azim's gaze flicked to him and then away again. 'I was kidnapped. I escaped. And now I'm here.'

'Those are the bones of the story, yes,' Malik answered. 'But there must be much more. Who kidnapped you? How did you escape? And why have you only come back now?'

Azim exhaled, a short, sharp release of breath. 'As far as I have been able to discern, a servant kidnapped me from the palace gardens, at the behest of a junior staff member of Enrico Salvas.'

'Salvas...' The name was familiar. 'Asad was negotiating with him,' Malik recalled slowly. 'A telecommunications deal...'

'Apparently he didn't like the terms,' Azim returned dryly. 'But the staffer acted without his knowledge. He didn't want to dirty his hands with a kidnapping. He had his employee dispose of me so he could claim he knew nothing about it.'

'Dispose of you?' Malik said, his stomach souring at the thought. 'How?'

'He left me in a slum in Naples, beaten to the point of unconsciousness. When I awoke, I'd been taken to a hospital and I couldn't remember my own name. I pieced together what I've just told you through research, not memory. I still don't remember that part of my life.'

Malik stared at him, appalled. For the first twelve years of his life his brother had been his confidant and closest friend. It hurt to think Azim might not remember any of it. 'When did you figure out who you were?'

'Only recently, when I saw a programme on the news about Alazar.' His gaze flicked away from Malik. 'They said Asad was dying and that you were going to be Sultan. The memories, or at least some of them, came flooding back. Some are gone for ever.'

Malik nodded slowly. 'So you have returned to Alazar to become Sultan. And just in time.'

Azim lifted his chin, his dark eyes glowing like banked coals. 'Yes, but I cannot do it alone.'

'You want my help?'

Azim shrugged. 'There is much I do not remember. I am a stranger in my own land.'

'Of course I will help you.' Malik knew there was no other response. 'Whatever it is you require.'

Azim gave a brief nod of acknowledgement. 'Thank you.' He paused, his expression turning shrewd. 'You will not miss being the heir?'

'No,' Malik answered frankly. He knew he meant it. 'In some ways, it will be a relief.' The sultanate had been thrust on him as a child, and he'd borne the burden dutifully, because he'd had to. But to be free of it? Free to do as he wished, live life as he wished...?

With no reason to marry Gracie. The realisation trickled coldly through him. Why would Gracie marry him now? Sam wasn't going to be Sultan. Malik didn't need an heir. Nothing was going to happen the way he'd thought, the way he'd insisted.

'I believe you are having second thoughts,' Azim observed coolly.

'Not...not about that.' Malik shook his head slowly; he felt dizzy, with each fresh realisation making him dizzier. He'd practically frogmarched Gracie to the altar; she'd be glad to leave. Sam would most assuredly be glad to return to Illinois. They would both have the freedom they craved. He'd made it abundantly clear he would never offer Gracie the kind of relationship he knew she really wanted. They didn't love each other. She'd been willing to make their marriage work because she'd had to, but if given a choice...

He couldn't bear the thought of her walking away from him, as his father once had, choosing to live apart rather than fight for the relationship. For *them.* He couldn't stand the possibility of seeing relief in her face when he told her she was free. And as for Sam...what would happen? Some custodial arrangement where Malik saw his son every six weeks? Summer holidays? He'd been counting on so much more.

He'd started to believe in the fairy tale, he realised, appalled at himself. He'd bought into the stupid dream. He'd been just as weak as his father, in so many ways, but at least he could be strong now. He could choose to walk away first.

'I will not dispute your claim, Azim,' he said quietly. Of that he was sure; he had no right, even if it meant losing Gracie. 'You are the oldest son. You are the rightful heir.'

'I'm glad you agree.'

'How could I not?'

'I thought you might have become used to the power. Accustomed to luxury.'

Malik cocked his head. 'You are angry with me.'

'No.' Azim flinched, rubbing his temples. It took Malik a few seconds to realise why.

'You're in pain,' he said. 'You're injured—'

'An old injury. It doesn't matter.' Azim dropped his hands as he shrugged aside Malik's words. 'I *am* angry,' he said as he stared out of the window at the landscaped gardens that fell away to undulating desert. 'But not at you. I'm angry at the villains who stole me from my own home. Angry that twenty years of my life have been wasted.'

'What have you been doing since...?'

Another shrug as Azim kept his gaze on the view. 'I crawled my way up from the pit. That is all you need to know.' He turned to Malik with a cold smile. 'And now I will reclaim my place, and my destiny as Alazar's Sultan.'

'Which is how it should be.' Even if it left Malik with nothing. With no one.

'You will break your engagement with Johara,' Azim instructed. 'She is meant to be Sultana, and she will be my bride now.'

'I have already broken it,' Malik answered, matching his brother's coolness. 'You do not need to dictate to me.'

Azim frowned. 'Why have you broken it? Is she damaged goods?'

'No, of course not.' Malik frowned at his brother's calculating tone. Azim had always been cut of a sterner cloth, but twenty years of suffering had made him almost unreachable, colder even than Asad. 'I was the damaged goods, if anyone.' He paused, hating to admit it even now. 'I'm infertile.'

Azim's expression did not change. 'I see.'

'I have a son, from an…an encounter ten years ago. I had intended to marry the mother, to make Sam legitimate.'

Azim nodded. 'And now?'

'Now it is not necessary.' He did not want to put it into words, and yet he knew he needed to. 'I shall send them both away.'

'Good. We will have to plan an announcement to make to the public as soon as possible. It is better for these things to be resolved.'

'Of course.'

Azim rose, and Malik followed suit. After a second's pause he made the correct obeisance and then watched his brother, the Sultan-in-Waiting, stride from the room.

Gracie paced the confines of the harem, her heart fluttering like a wild thing in her chest. Sam was sitting on the edge of the pool, kicking his bare feet in the water, his mouth pulled into a frown.

'So this guy is my uncle?' he asked after a moment, and Gracie let out an uncertain laugh.

'Yes, I suppose he is.'

'And he was *kidnapped*?'

'That's what your father told me.'

'So it's dangerous, being Sultan.'

'Oh, Sam.' Gracie sank onto the ledge next to Sam and

put an arm around his shoulders. 'Your father would always keep you safe.'

'I know, but...' Sam's lip jutted out. 'I like Alazar. And I like Illinois. I don't want everything to change so much.'

'I understand,' Gracie whispered. 'I feel the same, Sam, but couldn't it... Couldn't it be good for us all to be together? For you to have a proper dad?'

'Yeah.' Sam nodded slowly. 'Maybe.'

'Malik will come soon,' Gracie promised. 'And explain everything to us. You'll see, Sam, it will come all right.' She had to believe that. She had to put her trust in Malik, even though memories were storming through her, reminding her of another time when her world had been upended, and nothing had been as it had seemed. Then she'd learned Malik was Sultan-in-Waiting. What would she learn today?

The creak of a door split the silence like a crack of thunder, and then Gracie heard heavy footsteps. She turned to see Malik standing in the doorway to the pool area. His eyes were shadowed, his expression unreadable, with that awful impassivity Gracie had learned to dread. She scrambled to her feet.

'Malik—'

'We need to talk.'

'Okay,' Gracie said. Her heart was thundering now, her palms slick. Malik's tone hadn't been remotely encouraging. 'Sam...?'

'Stay here for a bit, Sam,' Malik said, and he gave his son a reassuring smile that didn't reach his eyes. 'I need to talk to your mother for a few minutes.'

Sam nodded uncertainly and Gracie followed Malik out of the pool area to the private sitting room.

'Malik, what's going on?' she asked as he closed the doors and then walked to the window, one arm braced against the ancient stone arch, his back to her. 'Azim is back…?'

'Yes. He didn't remember who he was until recently, when he saw my grandfather on the news. Apparently his memory came back then, and he made plans to return to Alazar.'

'Oh, my goodness…'

'He's going to be Sultan.' Malik's tone was flat.

Gracie blinked, taking his words in. 'Because he's the older brother,' she said slowly.

'Yes.'

So Malik would no longer be Sultan. Sam would no longer be his heir. The first rush of relief was chased by something far more menacing.

This changed everything—and yet nothing at all, because she still loved Malik. She still wanted to be with him—but did he want to be with her?

'So you can see,' Malik continued, his back still to her, 'that there is no longer any reason for us to marry.'

His words hit her like hammer blows. Gracie reeled back with the pain they caused. 'There isn't?' she managed in little more than a whisper. Why was she surprised? It had been the conclusion she had been painfully coming to herself, and yet…

'Surely you see that?' Malik turned around, his face as expressionless as ever, wiped clean of any betraying emotion. 'I no longer have any need to secure the succession. This is good news for you, Grace, is it not? You never really wanted to live in Alazar. Sam didn't want to be Sultan.'

'Don't,' Gracie said, her voice shaking, 'call me Grace.'

Malik stared at her, nonplussed. 'Why not?'

'Because you only call me that when you're trying to keep your distance,' she spat. 'And you can't withdraw from me now, Malik. Not when all this has happened. You can't just cut yourself off because it's convenient—'

'I'm merely stating facts.'

'Facts? What about what we've shared these last few days? What about *us*?'

Malik stared at her for a long moment. 'There is no us, Grace.'

'So all of it was meaningless? Manipulation to get what you wanted?' She felt as if she were being torn in half, all of her hopes dismantled, destroyed.

'It was enjoyable for both of us,' Malik dismissed. 'But you can't pretend you're not relieved. You didn't want to marry me. I couldn't offer you more children—'

'I didn't care about that—'

'You must have, a little.' She heard the pain in his voice, and everything in her ached.

'Malik—'

'You both came into this arrangement reluctantly,' Malik cut across her, his tone implacable. 'Now you can have your life back. So can Sam. And,' he finished with cutting precision, 'it isn't as if we loved each other.' He stared at her, daring her to disagree.

'No,' Gracie said slowly, not wanting to humiliate herself any further. 'It isn't as if we did.'

Malik stared at her for another awful beat before he drew himself up, his eyes cold, his mouth pressed into a hard line. 'Well, then. This works out best for everyone.'

Hurt coursed through her, a hot and unrelenting river. 'And what about Sam? What about him hearing yesterday that you're his father, and now you're walking out of his life? What do you think that will do to him?'

A muscle flickered in his jaw. 'I am not walking out of his life. I will visit…'

'Visits,' she scoffed, disbelieving and so very hurt. 'I

wasn't talking about visits,' she added, echoing Sam's words from the other day. 'I thought you were starting to care about your son, Malik. About...' *Me.* But even now, especially now, she couldn't say it. 'What am I to tell Sam?' she asked brokenly. 'That you've lost interest in him? Is that what you want me to say?'

Confusion marred Malik's features before his expression ironed out once more. 'I will tell him that things have changed. And I *will* come to see him. He can visit here. Plenty of fathers have the same arrangement, and it is perfectly acceptable.'

Gracie stared at him, at a loss, too devastated to hide how she felt. 'And this is what you want? Really?'

Malik lifted his steely gaze to hers. 'Yes.'

Gracie searched his face, trying to find some chink in his armour, some crack through which she could glimpse the man underneath, the man she'd once believed was there, who was waiting to realise he loved her. 'Why are you doing this?' Gracie asked quietly. 'Why does your brother's return have to make so much of a difference to us?'

'Because *us* was only a concept to secure the succession and ensure my country's stability,' Malik returned impatiently. 'You knew that, Grace.'

Gracie sagged. Why was she fighting him? Did she actually think she could argue him into caring? It was obvious, too obvious, that he didn't. He never had. He'd been intending to marry her for expediency's sake, and now he didn't have to.

'I thought more of you,' she said, each word distinct even as her voice trembled. 'I thought you were a better man than that. I thought you were a man who cared. Who... who loved.' Her voice choked and, drawing a shuddering breath, she lifted her chin. 'But clearly I was wrong. We'll be gone by morning.' And without bothering to wait for a reply, she left the salon and went in search of her son.

Malik stood by the window and watched as the sedan pulled up to the front of the palace. It was early morning, a bright new day, and Gracie and Sam were leaving for the airport shortly. Malik hadn't seen her since their awful conversation yesterday afternoon.

Her words had pinged around inside his head all night as he'd lain in bed, gritty-eyed and heavy-hearted. *I thought you were a better man than that. I thought you were a man who cared. Who loved.*

He'd made the choice to set her free, the choice not to love. Not to be weak. He'd felt it was the only choice he could make, because he hadn't wanted Gracie to make it first. Now, staring outside at the car that would take her away from him for ever, Malik wondered if he'd been wrong. What if she wouldn't have? *What if she'd told him she loved him?*

But she hadn't. She'd agreed with him that they hadn't loved each other, met his gaze unflinchingly all the while. It had been all the confirmation he ever could have wanted that he'd done the right thing. Made the right choice.

So why didn't he feel as if he had?

Malik drew a shuddering breath, fighting the urge to run downstairs and keep Gracie from going. He didn't move. He *was* doing the right thing. He had to be because the alternative was risking—what? His pride? His self-respect?

He'd acted, Malik realised with a hollow sensation in his gut, out of fear. Fear of being like his father, of being not just weak, but devastated by loving someone too much. He'd thought walking away was stronger, but what if he was more like his father in choosing that path? His father had walked away from him, from life, rather than face the possibility of risking again. Living and loving again. Was that what Malik was doing now? Was staying silent and letting Gracie go the cowardly choice?

The realisation slammed into him, leaving him breathless. He *loved* Gracie. He loved Sam. And he was letting them both walk out of his life because he was too much of a coward to fight, to risk both his pride and his heart.

The front doors of the palace opened and Malik watched as Gracie and Sam walked out. Gracie's arm was around Sam's shoulders, and the boy leaned into her, seeking both her comfort and strength. Gracie's face was pale but composed; she was far stronger than she'd ever given herself credit for. Malik's heart gave a wrench and he gasped aloud from the pain of it. He could not let this happen. He could not let Gracie walk out of his life a second time while he stood aside for duty's sake.

Drawing a deep, searing breath into his lungs, Malik turned from the window and sprinted down the stairs. By the time he reached the entrance to the palace, the car with Sam and Gracie had already driven through the gates. They were gone.

Malik stood there for a moment, his chest heaving, his heart breaking into fresh and jagged splinters. From behind him he heard footsteps.

'You care about her. The American.'

Malik turned slowly, his shoulders sagging. He felt as if the life force had drained from his body. He glanced at Azim, who watched him impassively from the front steps of the palace. 'Yes,' he said heavily. 'I care about her.' He swallowed. 'I love her.' The words did not, as he once would have expected, make him feel weak. They made him feel strong. He'd thought needing Gracie had been weakness, but now he saw it as strength. With her by his side he could do anything. *They* could do anything, together.

'Then why did you make her go?' Azim asked.

Malik closed his eyes briefly. 'I don't know. I was a fool. A frightened fool. We were only to marry for the sake of the kingdom, the sultanate. With that gone...' He released a long, low breath. 'I wasn't sure there was a point any more. Whether she would think that there was a point.'

'And you did not ask her?'

'No.' Malik rubbed his hand over his face. 'What can I offer now? I am not Sultan, I cannot give her children...'

Azim said nothing for a long moment. 'If she cares for you, perhaps those things won't matter.'

The last person Malik would have expected to receive relationship advice from was his brother. Azim's voice had been toneless, his face unreadable. He did not appear moved by Malik's predicament; he looked as if he felt nothing at all, and solving this situation was simply part of his role as the next sultan.

But Malik felt. He felt, with painful and shocking intensity, a hope for the future he and Gracie could still have. A future based not on expediency and convenience, but love.

'You're right,' he said as he strode past Azim into the palace. 'I need to tell her how I really feel.'

There was no royal jet this time, so Gracie and Sam waited in the small, airless lounge of Teruk's airport for the economy flight to Chicago. With three layovers it was going to take nearly thirty-six hours to reach home.

Sam had been silent and sullen since Gracie had told him they were going back to Illinois.

'What happened?' he'd asked. 'What about... What about my dad?'

Gracie had felt as if her heart were cracking right down the middle as she'd answered, 'He's staying here. But maybe he'll visit us back in America.'

Sam had stared at her, stricken. 'Maybe?' he'd repeated, and Gracie had wished she could be more certain.

'He still cares about you, Sam, of course he does. But now that his brother has returned, Malik won't be Sultan any more. You won't be Sultan.' She'd managed a wobbly smile. 'That's sort of a good thing, isn't it? Because you weren't so sure about that part.'

'I know.' Sam kicked at the floor with the toe of his sneaker. 'I didn't like that part. But I liked...I liked the dad part.'

'Oh, Sam.'

This felt wrong in so many ways. Why was Malik doing this to them? Why was he hurting everyone, maybe even himself?

Still wishful thinking, Gracie, she reminded herself. Malik had made it abundantly clear he didn't care about her.

How could she have, after trying to be so careful, let Malik al Bahjat break her heart a second time, and this so much worse than before? She felt as if her heart had been ground into dust, impossible to piece together again.

The airline steward called for them to board and with leaden limbs Gracie rose from her seat and shepherded Sam towards the gate for boarding.

'Gracie.'

For a moment she thought she'd imagined the voice. She tensed, not daring to hope. Then again, commanding this time. The voice of a sultan. *'Gracie.'*

Sam spun around. 'Dad!'

Slowly Gracie turned. Malik stood there, people drawing back in amazement as they recognised one of the Princes of the realm.

'What are you doing here?' she whispered.

'Looking for you. And Sam.' Malik's eyes burned silver fire as he looked at them both. 'I made such a mistake.'

'We can't talk here.' Gracie was conscious of all the curious stares, the straining ears.

'If His Highness would like a private room…' an airport official murmured, and Malik nodded his assent. Moments later they were ensconced in a small room with a table and chairs. They all stood, staring at each other, no one daring to speak first. And then Malik did.

'Gracie, I'm sorry,' he said in a low voice. He looked dishevelled, his clothes in disarray, his hair ruffled as if he'd raked his hand through it repeatedly. He looked wonderful. 'I'm sorry to you as well, Sam. I hurt you both and I wish I never had.'

'Malik…' Gracie began, and then found she couldn't say anything else. Her heart was too full, brimming with both hope and fear, even now.

'I should never have sent you away,' Malik said. He took a step towards her, his hands outstretched, palms upwards like a supplicant. 'I was afraid,' Malik said. 'I thought I was acting out of strength, because my father loved and was weak. My grandfather always told me that love made you weak, opened you to pain. And it does. Because I've never felt pain like the pain of losing you, Gracie.' He glanced at his son, his eyes damp. 'And you, Sam. That's the worst pain I've ever known.'

'It was the worst pain for me, too,' Gracie whispered. She felt near tears and she gulped them back. 'I don't care if you're Sultan, Malik—'

'And neither do I,' Sam chimed in. 'I just want you to be my dad.'

'That's what I want to be.' He took a deep breath, his eyes shining as he turned to Gracie. 'And your husband. I love you, Gracie, so much. And I love you, Sam. I want to share my life with you, if you'll let me. If you'll have me.'

'Oh, Malik.' Tears spilled down Gracie's face as she went to him, putting her arms around him.

He pulled her into a tight embrace, his lips against her hair as he whispered, 'I'm desperately, madly in love with you, Gracie Jones. Please say you'll have me.'

'Of course I will.'

'Even though I'm not Sultan? Even though there won't be any more children?' he whispered, and she heard a note of vulnerability in his voice that made her ache.

'All I want is you,' she assured him. 'You're all I'll ever need. You and Sam.'

Malik lifted his head to look at Sam, who was watching them both. 'And will you have me, Sam?' he asked seriously. 'As your father? As your dad?'

Wordlessly Sam nodded, and then he catapulted himself towards them both, squeezing into the best hug Gracie had ever had. They were finally and truly a family, and for Gracie it was the best feeling in the world.

* * * * *

If you enjoyed the first part of
Kate Hewitt's SEDUCED BY A SHEIKH *duet,*
look out for the second instalment,
THE FORCED BRIDE OF ALAZAR
Available May 2017!

Also, why not explore these other
Kate Hewitt titles
A DI SIONE FOR THE GREEK'S PLEASURE
DEMETRIOU DEMANDS HIS CHILD
MORETTI'S MARRIAGE COMMAND
INHERITED BY FERRANTI
Available now!

MILLS & BOON®
Hardback – April 2017

ROMANCE

The Italian's One-Night Baby	Lynne Graham
The Desert King's Captive Bride	Annie West
Once a Moretti Wife	Michelle Smart
The Boss's Nine-Month Negotiation	Maya Blake
The Secret Heir of Alazar	Kate Hewitt
Crowned for the Drakon Legacy	Tara Pammi
His Mistress with Two Secrets	Dani Collins
The Argentinian's Virgin Conquest	Bella Frances
Stranded with the Secret Billionaire	Marion Lennox
Reunited by a Baby Bombshell	Barbara Hannay
The Spanish Tycoon's Takeover	Michelle Douglas
Miss Prim and the Maverick Millionaire	Nina Singh
Their One Night Baby	Carol Marinelli
Forbidden to the Playboy Surgeon	Fiona Lowe
A Mother to Make a Family	Emily Forbes
The Nurse's Baby Secret	Janice Lynn
The Boss Who Stole Her Heart	Jennifer Taylor
Reunited by Their Pregnancy Surprise	Louisa Heaton
The Ten-Day Baby Takeover	Karen Booth
Expecting the Billionaire's Baby	Andrea Laurence

MILLS & BOON®
Large Print – April 2017

ROMANCE

HISTORICAL

MEDICAL

MILLS & BOON®
Hardback – May 2017

ROMANCE

The Sheikh's Bought Wife	Sharon Kendrick
The Innocent's Shameful Secret	Sara Craven
The Magnate's Tempestuous Marriage	Miranda Lee
The Forced Bride of Alazar	Kate Hewitt
Bound by the Sultan's Baby	Carol Marinelli
Blackmailed Down the Aisle	Louise Fuller
Di Marcello's Secret Son	Rachael Thomas
The Italian's Vengeful Seduction	Bella Frances
Conveniently Wed to the Greek	Kandy Shepherd
His Shy Cinderella	Kate Hardy
Falling for the Rebel Princess	Ellie Darkins
Claimed by the Wealthy Magnate	Nina Milne
Mummy, Nurse...Duchess?	Kate Hardy
Falling for the Foster Mum	Karin Baine
The Doctor and the Princess	Scarlet Wilson
Miracle for the Neurosurgeon	Lynne Marshall
English Rose for the Sicilian Doc	Annie Claydon
Engaged to the Doctor Sheikh	Meredith Webber
The Marriage Contract	Kat Cantrell
Triplets for the Texan	Janice Maynard

MILLS & BOON®
Large Print – May 2017

ROMANCE

A Deal for the Di Sione Ring	Jennifer Hayward
The Italian's Pregnant Virgin	Maisey Yates
A Dangerous Taste of Passion	Anne Mather
Bought to Carry His Heir	Jane Porter
Married for the Greek's Convenience	Michelle Smart
Bound by His Desert Diamond	Andie Brock
A Child Claimed by Gold	Rachael Thomas
Her New Year Baby Secret	Jessica Gilmore
Slow Dance with the Best Man	Sophie Pembroke
The Prince's Convenient Proposal	Barbara Hannay
The Tycoon's Reluctant Cinderella	Therese Beharrie

HISTORICAL

The Wedding Game	Christine Morrill
Secrets of the Marriage Bed	Ann Lethbridge
Compromising the Duke's Daughter	Mary Brendan
In Bed with the Viking Warrior	Harper St. George
Married to Her Enemy	Jenni Fletcher

MEDICAL

The Nurse's Christmas Gift	Tina Beckett
The Midwife's Pregnancy Miracle	Kate Hardy
Their First Family Christmas	Alison Roberts
The Nightshift Before Christmas	Annie O'Neil
It Started at Christmas...	Janice Lynn
Unwrapped by the Duke	Amy Ruttan